SAINTS

SAINTS AND SINNERS DUET BOOK 1

SOPHIA HENRY

KRASIVO CREATIVE

Cover Design: Amanda Shepard, Shepard Originals
Cover Photograph: Wander Aguiar, Wander Aguiar Photography
Cover Model: Zack Salaun
Editing by: Jenn Wood, All About the Edits
Proofreading by: Jackie Ferrell

"Every saint has a past, and every sinner has a future."
~ Oscar Wilde, A Woman of No Importance

#BeKindLoveHard

* * *

CONNECT with Sophia:
SophiaHenry.com

PATREON
INSTAGRAM
AMAZON
BOOKBUB

PROLOGUE
STASYA

Moscow

Dmitri Morozov is dead to me.

*C*onsidering our history, it should be an easy decision to make, but today's interaction sealed my hatred.

When I reach the Metro, I rush down the stairs with tears still streaming down my face. The platform is so congested, I have to elbow my way through the doors. There will be another one in a few minutes, but it's Friday night and waiting won't make a difference. Either way, I'll be fighting the crowd; the people wearing drab, gray work clothes, on their way home for the day, or those with slight pops of color, dressed up to go out for the evening.

Maybe that's what *I* should do. When I get home, I should get dressed up, call Svetlana, and ask her to meet me at the discotheque. Maybe letting loose to Victor Tsoi's latest song is just what I need to help me drown away the pain of Dima's cold

I

indifference when I asked him if he knew about my brother's defection to America.

The train jolts abruptly before heaving forward as it leaves the station. I plant my feet firmly for balance and tighten my grip on the bar overhead.

I haven't stopped crying since I left the Central Scarlet Army's hockey training base. Thankfully, anyone who's glanced my way has quickly averted their gaze. I close my eyes and take a deep breath, wiping away tears with the back of my free hand.

All I wanted was some answers. My twin brother, Vanya, who has shared everything with me since the womb, defected to the United States after a tournament in Sweden. Despite us being so close, he never uttered one word about it before he left. I thought going to Dima, his best friend on the team, would help me understand how my brother could have kept such a huge secret from me.

But the arrogant coward refused to reveal what he knew.

They were roommates. Friends! Was he not concerned or—at the very least—*inquisitive* when Vanya packed his bags and left?

Dima said he's scared. *He's* scared.

My family is being treated like criminals—being followed and questioned by the KGB—because of Vanya's desertion, and *Dima* is scared.

To be afraid is normal, but when a lieutenant in the military is a coward? That's unacceptable. Those in a position of power who have the ability to help must rise up. Though there may have been a time when I had feelings for him, I have no use for a chicken like him in my life.

When the train stops at *Aviamotornaya* station, I feel so numb and disoriented, it's as if the crowd is carrying me out the doors and up the stairs. I've walked home from here so many times, I do it on autopilot.

Vanya used to scold me for walking alone because the streets have gotten colder and darker over the last few years. He wasn't concerned about the weather or season, but the criminals and the violence they bring.

Mafia is everywhere, but I'm not scared. Gangs kill for money, power, and greed. They want something that someone else has.

I have nothing.

Besides, the *Bratva* is the least of my concerns. I have more to fear right in my own home. Ever since Mama died, I've become the lone target of my father's anger and violence.

Vanya's hockey accomplishments were the only bright moments in our mundane conversations. Now, we have nothing —just the bleak reality that he left us all behind.

For years, my brother swore he'd take me with him if he ever got the chance to live in America. He promised me again just a few weeks ago, minutes before he left for his most recent hockey tournament.

And now he's gone. And I'm here, stuck amid chaos and instability unlike anything I've ever lived through before in Russia.

At least life under communism was stable—boring, but stable.

The KGB has already harassed Papa, *Babushka*, and half of the other families who live in our apartment, asking them what they knew about Vanya's defection. It's only a matter of time before they come for me.

The thought of a KGB interrogation makes my stomach lurch. Though I rarely drink, I may join my father at the table with a glass of vodka tonight. I need something to numb the anger, betrayal, and heartbreak stewing for Vanya.

The concentrated gasoline smell permeates the air. I've gotten so used to the influx of vehicles taking to the roads over the last few years, I don't usually notice. But today, anxiety has my sensitive stomach bubbling with every inhale.

I've just crossed *Aviamotornaya Ulitsa* when, out of the corner of my eye, I notice a rusty Vaz creeping up the street. My jaw twitches involuntarily. Feeling a bit stupid for being nervous of an old car, I nuzzle my chin into my scarf and keep my gaze forward until it passes.

The loud rev of an engine makes me jump, and a shiny, black sedan speeds past and screeches to a stop a few meters ahead of me. My legs shake and I stumble over an uneven crack in the sidewalk.

Vaz is a common brand here, but black BMWs are only driven by mafia. Being stuck in the middle of crossfire between two gangs was not how I expected the day to end. But it's also not a surprise considering how the rest of it has gone.

I hold my breath, watching intensely as the sedan's driver and passenger doors fling open at the same time. Two men covered in black head-to-toe jump out and sprint toward me. My heart thumps in beat with their heavy footsteps pounding the concrete, each step getting louder as they get closer.

Swallowing back fear, I increase my speed and move to the side, giving the men space to get wherever they're going.

Suddenly, the taller of the two clasps his thick arms around me and starts carrying me toward the car. The other crouches down, grabs the bag I dropped, and sprints to the driver's side.

"No!" I scream as I kick my feet and fight to free myself. "Stop!"

It's a futile effort. There's no one on the road other than the Vaz, and the people inside know better than to try to stop mafia.

I stretch my legs to the ground, dragging my feet in an attempt to slow him down, but instead of having any effect, my shoes scrape against the sidewalk and one falls off. He tightens his grip and lifts me into the air.

When we get to the car, he yanks the door open and shoves me in face-first before slamming the door shut. It jars my feet, propelling my body forward and sending my cheek sliding across the seat.

"Please!" I cry out. "Please don't do this!" My clammy palms slip on the leather as I try to claw myself upright.

Instead of responding, the passenger spins around and leans forward. Cold sweat beads on my forehead as I scramble backward, pressing my spine against the seat. He wedges himself between the two front seats, grabs a fistful of hair, and pulls me toward him. I shake my head violently, but his grip doesn't loosen, and my jerky movements only enhance the pain.

He deftly wraps rope around my wrists, pulling it tight before making a complicated knot. When he's finished, he looks up. Icy blue eyes peer at me through the opening of the black balaclava masking his face.

When I gasp, he slams a foul-smelling rag against my mouth and I involuntarily ingest whatever's on the cloth. Only one thought runs through my head before everything goes black.

I know those eyes.

1

STASYA

ONE MONTH EARLIER

"Come on, Stasya!" Vanya calls to me as we hurry across the slick sidewalks between our apartment to the metro station. "Why are you so slow today?"

"I'm going as fast as I can, *Lieutenant*!" I snap at my brother, using his official military title as I reposition his hefty duffle bag on my shoulder. Thankfully, my heels act as picks, sticking into the softening ice and helping me keep my balance. "Did you pack extra so this thing would be heavier?"

"Technically, you wouldn't be permitted to speak to your commanding officer like that, but I'll let it slide since you're a civilian." While he chuckles at his own humor, I roll my eyes. "You lost the bet. You are my slave for the day."

"Of all the stupid ideas..." I mumble under my breath.

Normally, I wouldn't be so annoyed by my brother's teasing, but today is different because having to carry this heavy bag of hockey shit is my own fault. I'm the one who picked the terms of the silly bet I didn't think I'd lose.

"Do you think there will be someone to wait on me hand and foot when I'm in Detroit, Stasya?" he muses aloud. "Someone who will carry my gear and drive me to games?"

"Yes," I remind him. "*Me!*"

In January, Vanya found out he was selected by the Detroit team in last year's National Hockey League draft, and he hasn't stopped talking to me about it. I'm one of the only people he can talk to about his dreams of playing in America. Chances are, he'll never get to go because the USSR will never allow him to leave.

My brother is no stranger to being selected to play for elite leagues. Three years ago, the Central Scarlet Army—CSA—chose him to play on their hockey team—which is a great honor.

Leading up to it, he trained in the CSA junior system, but not every man who goes through the program makes the team —only the best of the best. Since then, he's spent eleven months out of the year with his team at the training base. He gets one weekend away from the *baza* a month—*if* he's lucky. Most of the time, he doesn't even get that break.

But that's the price he proudly pays to represent our country playing hockey for the Scarlet Army.

Honestly, my heart hurts for him. A team from the best hockey league in the world selected him to play for them, but we both know it's impossible for him to leave the Soviet Union right now. As a member of CSA, he's an officer in the military who's job is to play hockey, and he's bound by a contract. If he were to leave, he would be classified as a deserter, and punished with death if he ever came back.

There has been so much turmoil and uncertainty here since

Gorbachev's *perestroika* that no one thinks too brightly about what the future holds right now. Then again, many of us Russians don't think too brightly about the past either.

The promise of even more change and uncertainty hovers in the air, thick as a blanket of winter snow over the city. The restructuring was supposed to be good for the Soviet Union.

Glasnost—more openness and transparency in the government—was supposed to bring prosperity and freedom like the people of the Soviet Union hadn't experienced in almost a century. Instead of everything being run by the government, individuals could open businesses.

We were told we would be able to buy goods and foods we'd never had access to before. We would have more freedom! We would be like the rest of Europe!

It all sounds wonderful. Yet, we're still standing in line for the most basic goods—bread, eggs, sugar.

And who could afford to start a business?

The people who were already making money—criminals.

Vanya's silence is uncharacteristic.

I narrow my eyes and kick a clump of packed, dirty snow lingering from the last snowfall. "If you get the opportunity to live in America, you must take me with you, Vanya. You remember your promise, yes?"

The snow hits his calf and breaks apart, but it doesn't affect him. He looks at me over his shoulder with soft eyes. "I haven't forgotten, Stasya. I'd never forget about you."

Maybe—in the grand scheme of life—he wouldn't leave me behind, but right now it seems like he's trying his best. He's walking so fast, I have to jog to keep up. Which is close to impossible for me. I'm dressed for work, and this thigh hugging skirt and high heels are not ideal for running through the snow and slush while hauling a heavy hockey bag.

"Are you excited about the tournament?" I ask, changing the subject. There's no reason to waste time on dreams about a life in America that will most likely never happen.

"Of course," he answers quickly. "But Stockholm just got hit with a huge snowstorm, so that's not good. I was hoping for nicer weather than we have here."

"I wish I could go with you," I say longingly, dismissing his annoyance over some snow.

I'm very excited for my brother, but I envy all the travel he gets to do with his hockey team. I never thought much about traveling before Vanya started going to tournaments all over the world.

Growing up, we took trips to Leningrad and visited family and friends outside of Moscow. We spent every summer weekend at our *dacha*, the tiny country house *Babushka's* father built in Ramenskoye, but I've never been anywhere outside of the Soviet Union.

Why would I need to? We have everything we need right here.

Or so I thought.

Until recently, I didn't realize we were missing out. The government provides us everything we need from housing, healthcare, and food right down to clothing and shoes. Maybe the fashions aren't that great, but thankfully *Babushka* taught me how to sew when I was young.

Ever since then, I took on the task of making clothing for my family. It's easy for me now and I enjoy it. Knowing I can make dresses for me and my grandmother out of Papa's old shirts and thick, waterproof coats out of Vanya's old duffle bags gives me a sense of pride.

People have even noticed my clothes. Marina Smirnova, one

of my co-workers at Gosbank, the state-run bank of the Soviet Union, said my designs could be in a store one day.

The way she says it makes me think she means a store in a fashion capital like New York or London, not one of the ones we're forced to shop in which are filled with drab colors and boring patterns.

She's even asked me to make her a few things. Knowing she thinks highly of my work makes me feel good.

Though communism is the butt of most of our jokes, and many older people complain about how we live, I never thought there was any other way since it's the only thing I've ever known.

When our leaders began to change policies from the way things have been done for more than seventy years to restructure and reform to create a more open market, it made me wonder what was so great about communism in the first place and why we'd been led to believe it was the only way for so long.

Vanya always came home raving about music and fashions commonly found in the West—songs we'd never heard or things we never had the opportunity to buy until very recently, at outrageous prices. People there got to choose everything from where they worked and lived right down to the color of their shoes.

And there was so much to choose from! The stories he told me about other countries, especially the United States, were straight out of a Utopian dream and gave me an itch.

Now, I dream about wearing fabrics and clothing in different patterns and styles from what everyone else is wearing. I long to travel out of the country so badly I can taste it.

Sometimes, while at work, I daydream of taking a holiday in Rome or Paris, sitting outside at a café, sketching the clothing designs constantly swirling through my head as a sip a fancy coffee drink.

But it's not possible right now.

Even if I did see something I liked that wasn't Soviet manufactured, I could never buy it. The small amount of money I make goes to my family. We are a unit who always looks out for each other's best interest before giving in to selfish desires.

We'd already heard from family members who live outside of the city that food and goods were being rationed and shelves were empty, but the shortages hadn't hit us in Moscow yet—until recently.

The first time I complained about standing in line for bread, *Babushka* reminded me of how things were when she was a child during The Great War. She lived through years of rationing and even a few months where she and her family almost starved. I believed my grandmother because I'd studied that part of our country's history, but it was a concept I could never comprehend until now.

Since that moment, we've been stocking up on foods that will last, and saving the rest of our money. It's certainly smarter to save for the uncertain future, then to waste it on something frivolous—like blue jeans or a vinyl record from America.

There's a big difference between *needs* and *wants*. We have everything we need right now. Maybe in the new Russia, we'll have some of the things we want.

There's too much unrest. Too much change. Too much worry. Papa says everything we know will be different within a few years—and I believe him.

All we can do is wait.

As we walk, a gust of frigid air sends chills straight through my threadbare winter coat, numbing my entire body. Tears prick at my eyes, so I lower my head and snuggle my chin underneath my handmade scarf.

Crossing the street without looking up isn't the smartest idea, since Moscow drivers are crazy, but I trust Vanya won't lead me into oncoming traffic.

I've made it across the street, but I trip on the curb and fall right into something.

Thankfully, it's a human, rather than a car.

Strong hands grab onto my shoulders, keeping me from falling face-first into the snow.

When I look up, I'm staring into the soft, brown eyes that danced through my dreams since the moment we meet—until recently.

Dmitri Morozov—Dima to those of us close to him—one of Vanya's teammates, is the type of man you can't get out of your head. His dark, curly hair and sexy bedroom eyes put me under a spell, lulling me into believing I may have had the wrong idea about Siberians all these years.

Maybe they were a magical and mystical group uplifted by the bleak, desolate landscape fitting for prisons and labor camps.

Vanya has always said I live with my head in the clouds. And maybe I do. Instead of seeing people for who they are, I see them how I think they could be in the very best light. I don't think it's a bad thing to want people to be their best selves, but I end up disappointed.

Maybe that's from growing up the way we did. With the exception of my brother and childhood friend who lived in our building and came to my aid on many occasions, I didn't have many heroes in my life.

I haven't met many people from anywhere other than Moscow or Leningrad, so the mystery of Dima being from the far east was part of his charm. Had I been thinking with my head instead of my heart, I may have realized Dima would be like Siberia itself—wild and cold.

During the times Vanya actually gets a chance to come home, all of our friends hang out together. It wasn't unusual for his teammates to stay with us for the weekend. Very few are from the Moscow metro area, and would never be able to make it home and back before they had to be at the base again.

This year, we had four members of Vanya's team staying with us on New Year's Day, the most celebrated holiday in Russia. More people are always welcome, but the extra bodies made for tight sleeping arrangements. Thankfully, we're lucky to live in an apartment with families who love to celebrate and welcome friends, and would make sure everyone had a place to rest.

Holiday enchantment had everyone in the apartment giddy. We moved from room to room, eating New Year's staples like tangerines, Olivier salad, and jellied meats while drinking vodka and toasting to the new year.

The mix of excitement and too much alcohol had my hormones raging and my thoughts swirling about how Dima and I could be alone.

After a few hot and heavy kisses, we devised a plan to get away from the crowd. I would go to bed first, complaining that the vodka did me in, and he would follow shortly after. Nothing could have stopped us, not even the fact that my entire family sleeps in the same room—and I share a bed with my brother.

While I can't say losing my virginity was life-changing, the fast and fumbling experience wasn't horrible either.

We finished well before any of our friends and family retired for the night. Dima slipped out a few minutes after. I was upset, until he assured me he'd love to stay and hold me, but it made more sense to get back to the party before people started talking.

Amid the music and laughter, I drifted off to sleep with a full heart and a satisfied smile on my lips.

The next morning, Dima acted as if nothing ever happened. And I mean *nothing*.

He was cold and refused to speak to me—as if the year we'd spent getting to know each other never happened. As if the moment we shared just hours before never happened. I pretended like I wasn't affected, but his indifference stung me to the core.

I still hung out with Vanya and his friends when they came home, but when Dima stayed with us, I'd go out with my friends instead of hang out with my brother. I hated making the choice because I missed Vanya terribly, but I didn't want to be around Dima.

Evidently, the feeling was mutual, because in the rare times I did see him, he didn't speak to me and barely even looked at me. Normally, he stayed as far away as possible, but a few times I caught him looking my way when he had another girl in his arms. Which reinforced what a pig he was.

"Sorry. I— I wasn't looking," I stammer. My heart beats rapidly betraying my quest for indifference.

He looks past me, toward Vanya, and his entire demeanor changes. The warm eyes that greeted me initially turn frigid as the Moscow air and his square jaw tightens. "You need to watch where you're going when you cross the road," he snarls.

"You have no right," I say, jerking out of his grasp and hurrying toward my brother. Once I've caught up, I drop his heavy bag in the snow at his feet.

The nerve of Dima to be angry with me. *He's* the one who led *me* on—showering me with sweet words and sexy smiles for months. He certainly had me fooled into thinking he liked me. When that magical moment came for us to be together, when *he* crawled into *my* bed, I thought we had something that would last. He should be ashamed to look me in the eye, let alone speak to me, with such an angry tone.

"Stasya!" Vanya scowls and scoops up his bag, throwing the strap over his shoulder as if it weighs nothing. When he looks up, he sees Dima and sighs. "Don't start with the drama."

My brother knows all the details of what happened between Dima and I since he's heard it from both sides. It annoys me that he stays neutral. I don't care if it's his line mate and close friend—I'm his sister. He should always take my side.

Then again, he has to be stuck with Dima for eleven months of the year and relies on him for much of his hockey success, so I should be understanding of that.

"Vanya!" Dima greets my brother by placing his hands on his shoulders and leaning in to kiss his cheeks. "It's been too long!"

"Two full days is longer than we had last month, as I recall." Vanya laughs.

"Dima sees you more than I do," I pout, feeling invisible and left out.

My brother rolls his eyes. "You hate me when I'm home and love me when I'm gone."

"That's how it supposed to be between siblings, yes?" Dima leans over, looking toward the entrance to the metro, as if they might miss their train. "We should go."

"I'm allowed to complain," I say, following them down the stairs. "I don't get to fly to Sweden today. When I get off the train, I'll be walking to work in the cold by myself."

"What!" Vanya stops abruptly and spins around. "You know it's not safe to be out here alone."

"I'll be fine," I say, mentally chastising myself. I hadn't meant to slip up and tell him. There's no reason to get him worked up worrying about me.

"I thought Nikolai was meeting you here for the train?"

"The market called him about bread, but he's in line waiting for anything he can get. Which won't be much since the shelves are bare."

"If you don't start listening, you're going to get killed. That's the Moscow we live in now."

"I'm not worried about Moscow killing me, Vanya. I'm worried about Papa doing it," I whisper.

Vanya grabs me and pulls me into his arms, hugging me tightly. We both know there's truth behind my words.

Tears prick at my eyes, as they do every time he leaves. Over the last twenty years, Vanya and I have shared everything. Despite our teasing, I'll miss my brother fiercely. Though he's only four minutes older than I am, he's always been my protector. Without him, I have no one to shield me from Papa's anger —or his friends—who have gotten seedier since Mama died.

"I will never leave you, Stasya." Vanya rests his cheek on top of my head. "I have a plan, but you must trust me. Have I ever let you down?"

"Never."

Vanya is the only constant in my life—the person who will always look out for me and never let me down.

2

KIRYA

I've done a lot of crazy things in my life, but helping someone defect might go down as the craziest. And that's coming from someone who's committed and witnessed thousands of crimes.

Though the plan to have Ivan Kravtsov, defect from the USSR to America during the World Ice Hockey Championship has been months in the making, it's still nerve-wracking.

The pulsing in my locked jaw reminds me of how much pressure I'm under.

There are so many moving pieces that need to fall into place, and we were limited to what we could do before the actual event. One thing is certain, getting him out of the team hotel without any one on the Central Scarlet Army organization noticing is going to be one of the most challenging parts.

Once Vanya makes it to America, he'll be fine. But if anything goes wrong from now until the plane from Stockholm to New York takes off, we're going to have to think quick.

And by "we" I mean "me." I'm the one who created the plan, did the research, and contacted every single human I knew who could help us pull this off.

If we get caught, we'll all get into major trouble. The Americans would be jailed, but Vanya and I would get a one-way ticket to the firing squad.

The tournament is over.

The USSR won.

They haven't yet realized what they're about to lose.

Vanya and I are huddled with two representatives of the Detroit hockey team in the lobby of the hotel where the teams in the tournament have been staying over the last two weeks.

"Who are you again?" Chris Brookins, the Chargers Assistant General Manager asks, peering at me over round, wire-rimmed glasses.

The tall, thick man was known an enforcer when he played in the seventies. Though he seems like he could hold his own, he's smart to be wary.

Detroit must really want Vanya, because the fact that Americans have trusted a guy like me with their lives surprises the shit out of me. I thought they were all scared of the big, bad Russians.

"I am Kirill Antonov, his translator. I'm the one who's been communicating with Mallon, your reporter friend," I answer with complete confidence in my English. I've been studying the language for as long as I can remember.

After they'd drafted Vanya last June, the Chargers had to find a way to contact him, knowing the State would never let an NHL team offering money and freedom anywhere near their athletes. They asked Jack Mallon, a reporter from their local newspaper who learned Russian during his years in the military, to meet with Vanya while he was in Alaska covering another international hockey tournament.

Under the guise of writing a story about the Central Scarlet Army team, Mallon was allowed access to Vanya for an interview. Before he left, Jack presented him with a Chargers magazine, telling him that it would give him some information about the team. Inside was a letter from Detroit, letting Vanya know they would do everything in their power to bring him over whenever he decided he was ready to come to America.

But the letter was in English, and Vanya couldn't read it. Even without an understanding of the contents, he knew enough not to share it with his superiors. Since Vanya and I have been friends our entire lives, and he knew I spoke English, he came to me to translate.

Though we hadn't seen each other much since taking different paths in life as teenagers, when he called asking me to meet him, my only questions were: when and where?

At our meeting, he said he came to me because I was the only person he trusted that spoke English and would be excited to engage in something illegal and dangerous.

How could I say no after such flattery?

Once I explained what the letter from Detroit said, he agreed to leave the USSR without hesitation. His prompt decision made me see my old friend in a new light. I assumed he would blindly follow the Russian machine, but his courage surprised me.

We discussed what defection would mean for him as an Army officer. If he were caught, he would be considered a traitor, a criminal. A *light* sentence would be spending the rest of his life at a labor camp in Siberia. Most likely, he would be killed as soon as he reentered the country.

Being a product of the Russian hockey system serves him well when it comes to confidence because failing is never an option. To him, there were no consequences of his decision, only rewards. He said he'd seen the older guys on the team fight for too much to let the opportunity slide.

He never had the same mental investment in the Soviet system as they did because he grew up among political turbulence and instability. He came up in the system at the same time veteran players like Smirnov and Makarlov fought for better living conditions at the training base, more time off to spend with their wives and children, and the ability to go to America to play the game they loved.

Athletes will always bring money—they can be bought, sold, and marketed to bring in revenue. Why would Vanya do that in the Soviet Union where the corrupt State sports department would take the majority of the money and leave him poor? At least in the NHL, he would get to put the money he makes into his own bank account.

After our discussion, he asked me if I would contact Detroit and help him get the process started, and I agreed. Since then, Mallon and I have been communicating, acting as translators for our respective parties, to create a plan to get Vanya to Detroit.

Brookins glances at Vanya for confirmation, who has no clue what either of us just said, but he trusts me. I told him I'd help him get to America and I plan on keeping my promise.

The bustling lobby has my neck and shoulders tense. I'm aware of every person that passes. The team never travels out of the country without Sovietsport officials and KGB agents. There are multiple checks and balances to keep each athlete in line and accounted for. Once someone realizes Vanya isn't in his room, there will be an all-hands-on-deck search for their missing superstar. And it will go fast.

Though it was the Detroit organization's idea to steal Vanya away during the tournament, I can guarantee I have the most experience with shady situations out of the four of us standing here. The suits from the Chargers think I'm Vanya's translator friend, which is fine with me. They'd shit their designer pants if they knew about half of the things I've done.

Which is why I feel personally responsible for this plan working—and for everyone's safety.

Out of the corner of my eye, I notice a man looking at us for a second too long. The hair rises on the back of my neck, alerting me that he might be a problem.

Wasting time will get us all killed.

"We need to move this," I tell Brookins. "I think we were being followed."

"Fuck," he hisses, glancing at the man next to him, another member from the Detroit organization. "Of course we are. Where should we go?"

Sweat glistens above his eyebrows. He's nervous— and understandably so. The Chargers organization has spent too much money and put their asses on the line for Vanya to get caught.

I understand enough about the male ego to assume that when they agreed to do this, they probably had some romantic notion that it would be fun, like playing spies in a Hollywood movie.

The reality of helping someone defect—or any criminal activity—is a lot less glamorous.

I've seen it countless times with boys in Moscow, puffing out their chests and acting like big pines when they're just tiny trees, members of small street gangs with absolutely no authority. When they meet real mafia, they run away with piss darkening the crotch of their pants.

These two American men must be courageous or stupid, because what they are doing is against the law. They may think they're stealthy, but this will be all over the news in every country. And they're fucking with the Soviet government—the ultimate enemy. Maybe this is the final phase of the Cold War. Steal the Soviet Union's most prized possessions and watch the country crumble.

Money trumps everything—even politics. Detroit wants their draft pick and they'll do whatever it takes to get him, even if they have to bend international rules to steal him from another country.

"There is a mall at Hamngatan and Regeringsgatan called the Gallerian. When you get there, drive around to the back entrance on Jakobsgatan. We will meet you out there." My answer is quick and decisive because I've thought of everything.

We all knew KGB would be looking for Vanya as soon as the CSA coaches and trainers realized he wasn't in his room. In preparing for this moment, I researched Stockholm and the surrounding areas. Keeping Vanya safe is my number one priority and that meant having multiple backup plans in case we had to switch gears quickly.

"Perfect. We'll be there in twenty minutes." The men walk away quickly, finally comprehending that time is of the essence in a situation like this. Suddenly, Chris turns around and asks, "Is he certain he wants to do this? To come with us?"

"One hundred percent," I answer for Vanya before spinning around. We exit the hotel through a different door to avoid being seen leaving with the Americans.

Vanya left with only a few personal things in this possession. I brought extra clothes and hygiene products he'll need to get to America. Once he's there, someone from the team will take him shopping.

I wish I could go to Detroit with him, but I have a meeting with my uncle in Brooklyn, New York. I know he'll be fine when he gets to America, but Vanya is as close to a brother as I'll ever have and I'll always look out for his best interest.

Once we're on the street, we hail a cab and direct the driver to the Gallerian.

Vanya hasn't said two words since we left the hotel and his silence worries me. I understand having doubts and fear now that the moment is here, but this is where I need his courage. If I know anything about my friend, it's that he's a natural leader and a strong decision maker.

"Are you rethinking leaving for Detroit?" I ask.

"No." A thick patch of dark blond hair flops over his right eye as he shakes his head.

"Then what are you thinking about?" I hit his thigh with the back of my hand. "Your brain is working so hard, you have steam coming from your ears."

He's silent, chewing on his bottom lip for what seems like an hour, but of course it's only been a few seconds. It reminds me of when I would find his sister, Stasya, sitting on the floor in the common hallway in our communal apartment when we were young.

Every time her father beat her, she would flee to the hallway and wait for him to fall asleep. As if I had a sixth sense to feel her pain, I'd open the door of my family's room and find her with her back against the wall, wringing her hands and biting her bottom lip to keep from crying.

As children, we're taught that tears don't solve anything. That tears are weakness. Seeing her forcing herself to be stoic when I knew she wanted to break down is permanently imprinted in my mind.

Fuck living in a culture that allows men to beat their daughters, but doesn't allow the daughters to display emotion or be able to do anything about the abuse.

It's one of the reasons hate fuels my heart. It's one of the reasons I chose the path I did—to live outside the laws and rules of Soviet society.

I agreed to help Vanya defect because getting out of this country puts him on the path to a better life. As a teenager, I vowed to do anything in my power to push Russians toward the freedoms and life we deserve. I truly believe I was born to incite change. And I'll do it by any means necessary.

Though they are twins, I've never looked at Vanya and been reminded of his sister before. I see them as two completely different individuals.

Stasya was my first love.

First love. Only love. Lost love.

We spent our entire childhoods together. I was three years old when the Kravtsov twins were born. When you grow up in a communal apartment, your neighbors become closer than your extended family, whether you want them to be or not. There's no way to keep people out of your business, so it's better to give in and work as a unit—the Russian machine.

The *babushkas* watched the children while the parents worked. Or—in Vanya and Stasya's case—one parent worked. Their father just drank.

Sometimes our families combined our resources, sharing food and cooking meals together. My mother always contributed the fresh fish and meat her brother, Viktor, brought over to the apartment's multi-family dinners. Though Viktor didn't live with us, he was always around, caring for us and bringing us treats. He had connections no one else in our apartment had, and kept my family stocked with exotic foods and gifts.

As a boy growing up without a father, Uncle Vitya was my hero, my inspiration, the man I looked up to. He taught me everything; from how to ice skate to how to shoot a gun.

I listened intently when he talked about his ideals and gave me advice, soaking up everything he said like a sponge. Though he was a powerful man, and maintained close friendships with people in crucial administrative positions in the country, he denounced communism in favor of capitalism.

Which is why it wasn't surprising when I found out he was among the first people who started illegal businesses in the seventies. They created a black market that still thrives today. Growing up able to buy goods that weren't sold in government stores never seemed wrong or "illegal" to me. I wondered why there even needed to be a black market. Why couldn't all Russians have access to the things they sold there?

I understand Vanya's fear and uncertainty about defecting. It goes against the Soviet propaganda we've been brainwashed with our entire lives. Especially someone like Vanya, an officer in the Scarlet Army and a player on the most successful hockey teams of all time. Living in that environment for so long made the weight of his decision heavier because the costs of leaving were higher for him.

Most people didn't grow up with entrepreneurs like Uncle Vitya in their families, like I did. That's not to say everyone agreed with communism. On the contrary, Soviet society was wonderful fodder for humor.

The propaganda starts early in schools. I still remember Stasya, who couldn't have been more than seven years old at the time, walking home from school on a freezing, cold November day with her coat unbuttoned just to show off her badge—a shiny, red star with a gold Lenin face in the middle. She and Vanya must have had their "Little Octoberist" ceremony that day. Vanya hadn't seemed to care about the pin, but Stasya wore it proudly, beaming and strutting down the street.

It made me laugh at the time, but I couldn't break her heart by telling her. As people get older, they realize on their own that the propaganda is complete bullshit.

Vanya knows it, or he never would have set this plan into motion.

And he better open his fucking mouth soon, because he'll fuck up everything we've done so far if he's really as nervous as he seems.

I'll get the concerns out of him one way or another, even if I have to resort to unusual methods. I have a way of getting people to talk—and it has nothing to do with the special treats I used to offer Stasya. I don't have softness in my heart for many people like I had for her. Not even her brother.

"I'm worried about Stasya," he finally says.

My head snaps to him. I should have known. The uncanny sixth sense I have for her well-being must've brought the memories of her to my mind.

He pushes the hair out of his eyes only for it to fall right back and looks at me solemnly before speaking. "Investigators will think she knew about what I was planning, Kirya. They'll question her—harass her. We're too close. They won't believe that she didn't know."

He's right. The KGB will interrogate his entire family, but they'll focus on Stasya because of their relationship.

The moment he mentioned her name, my mind was made up—Stasya will never fear for her life.

I swore years ago that I would do anything in my power to

protect her, and I have a hell of a lot more power now than I did then.

I lock eyes with my friend. "She will be fine," I assure him. "You have my word."

Vanya nods and his shoulders relax in relief. He turns to the window and stares out at the bustling streets of Stockholm.

When the cab drops us off at the front of the mall on Hamngatan, I pay the driver quickly and usher Vanya to the doors. We wander around for a little while, going in and out of a few shops, trying to give the perception we're just two guys shopping, as we make our way to the doors near the back.

The chances that we weren't followed from the hotel to the mall are slim. Despite my lifestyle, I'm not used to being in a constant ultra-vigilant state, and the paranoia is getting to me.

I check my watch. "It's been over twenty minutes. We need to get to the back door and see if the car is here," I tell Vanya.

"Okay," he agrees. His hand shakes as he places a button-down, dress shirt back onto a rack. He's still more nervous than I've ever seen anyone and I wonder if we're even going to be able to pull this off.

I punch his shoulder, and he turns to me. "You can do this."

He nods and gives me two thumbs up.

Very reassuring. But I know the kid isn't a pussy, so I trust he'll buck up when he needs to.

Out of the corner of my eye, I see two large men in shabby, gray trench coats and sunglasses coming toward us. Their obvious inability to blend in would normally make me laugh, but I refrain. Our chances of escaping are much better knowing exactly who's after us.

"Follow me," I bark out the command. "Fast!"

Vanya and I wind through as many different racks as we can

to try to lose the men in pursuit. It won't be that easy, I know, but it seems to help.

As soon as we're out of the store, I see the large, double doors that lead to the back exit and bolt toward them. I'm grateful to be working with a world-class athlete because I don't have to worry about Vanya lagging behind. He passes me easily, making it to the doors and pushing them open before I even reach them.

As soon as we're outside, he points to Brookins standing next to a navy-blue car with the engine running.

The impact of the situation must be hitting him because the American who had a calm and cool demeanor earlier looks as white as a ghost.

When he sees us, he wastes no time opening the back door and ushering us in before jumping in himself. The driver hits the gas before he can even close the door.

"Do you think we're being followed?" Brookins' sidekick asks as we drive through the streets of Stockholm. I swear I wouldn't be able to remember the guy's name even if someone had a gun to my head.

"Absolutely," I answer dryly.

I didn't think it was possible for his face to lose any more color, but it drains a shade lighter. There's no reason to sugar-coat the situation for him. We won't be completely safe until the plane to New York is off the ground.

Brookins turns around and looks Vanya in the eye. "You can still go back if you want. This is your last chance to change your mind."

Before I can finish translating that he's entering the point of no return, he interjects, "No. I go."

With those three words, Ivan Kravtsov became the face of freedom for Soviets.

* * *

WHEN WE ARRIVE AT THE U.S. EMBASSY, VANYA AND I HAVE TO sneak inside wearing clothes borrowed from the Americans. The less we look like ourselves the better because embassies are always being watched.

Once we've made it inside, a sense of relief washes over me, even though I know we're not in the clear yet. Pulling the tattered, gray Boston College sweatshirt Brookins gave me over my head, I collapse into a chair and toss it onto the small coffee table next to me.

As I sit in the uncomfortable office chair, sipping stale coffee, I listen as they organize the paperwork Vanya will need to leave the country. Some of it was already here, like his NHL contract, which Detroit's owner had faxed over. The travel documents saying he signed would need to be drawn up today with both him and the Detroit representatives present.

A TV blares from the next room. I don't know Swedish, but I can clearly make out Ivan and USSR hockey. Vanya's disappearance being all over the Swedish news already doesn't bode well for us.

My knee shakes as more minutes tick by. I've never helped anyone defect before, so I'm no expert, but I understand enough about Soviet Union officials and the KGB to know the longer we're in Sweden, the less likely it is my friend will make it to North America without being apprehended.

While the Detroit representatives and the embassy agents work diligently on the documents, Vanya gets permission to call his family.

After pressing a few buttons, he pauses. His eyebrows veer together as he rattles off his home number and asks to be connected to Stasya. He puts his hand over the mouthpiece and says, "They put me on hold."

I swallow thickly and lean forward, wondering if having an operator dial out is the way all calls happen at the embassy. It seems odd that he can't call his family directly.

Suddenly, Vanya mouths the word, "Fuck," and slams the receiver onto the base.

"What happened?" I ask, jumping from my chair.

"It was not the same operator. It was someone asking questions," he says gravely his eyes meeting my worried gaze. "I think they know where we are. They are listening to calls."

"No more names," I snap. "If you make a phone call, we don't use names, got it?"

Vanya nods.

Brookins rises from his chair hastily and bounds toward us. "What's going on?" he asks, glancing from Vanya to me quickly as if we're concealing something from him.

"They're listening to calls," I explain. "Soviet government."

"I thought—the embassy—I—Jesus," the man stutters. He rubs his sweat-speckled face with both hands. "I really hope the paperwork is almost done. I'm ready for this to be over."

As he walks wearily back into the office, I stop an older woman passing in the hallway. "Excuse me?" I ask. "Can you tell me what they're saying on TV?"

"They're searching for a player from the Russian National Team. They say he's been kidnapped." Despite the news, she doesn't seem fazed.

I imagine she's seen a lot of things go down working at the American Embassy in Russia.

I sit down again, closing my eyes and leaning back in my chair, trying to get comfortable. Though I have a knack for being calm under fire, the stress of the situation has me on edge. I'm confident, but cautious.

I take a deep breath, letting the hum of bustling background noise and the cadence of Swedish speakers on TV lull me into relaxation.

Planning and executing the international defection of a Central Scarlet Army hockey player has to be at the top of the list when it comes to high level crimes. Sure, I had the money and assistance of a rich American organization, but I still did the work.

If I pull this off, it will prove to Uncle Vitya I'm ready for the next level. Since he never had children, I'm the closest he has to a son. I've spent more than ten years learning and hustling to prove I'm worthy of being his second-in-command.

Just by being related to him and accepting the gifts he gave me, I'd unknowingly become part of the criminal life. But I actually *chose* the life at thirteen, when I started hanging out in Red Square trading cheap Russian chocolates and matryoshkas, the nesting dolls foreigners love, to tourists visiting Moscow. People were eager to trade their jeans, vinyl records, even beauty products, for hokey Russian souvenirs. Once Uncle Vitya realized my knack for sales, he started supplying me with endless trinkets.

A few years later, he took my mother and I to America for the first time. That's when I was able to take my business to the next level, bringing home two suitcases full of things to sell on the black market.

I open an eye and glance at Vanya and the Detroit representatives, huddled over paperwork. All seems well, so I cross my arms over my chest and settle back again, relaxing in the satisfaction of how far I've come.

* * *

For as much drama as it was from the hotel to the Embassy, the drive from the Embassy to the airport is uneventful. But all four of us are on high alert because we know there's still time for something to go wrong.

Vanya and I walk around the airport in our ill-fitting, borrowed clothes until it's time to board. We don't want to sit in one place for too long, and we definitely don't want to be seen with the guys from the Chargers.

Over the course of my life, I've been in some intense situations—mugged, kidnapped, shot...but I've never breathed such a huge sigh of relief as I do when the airplane leaves the ground.

Ivan Kravtsov, a Lieutenant in the Scarlet Army, is officially a criminal—a traitor of the highest level.

And I can proudly say I helped him defect.

* * *

As soon as we step inside the terminal at JFK International Airport in New York City, reporters swarm us. I slip sunglasses on and pull the baseball cap over my eyes, trying to keep my identity concealed despite feeling like one of those asshole KGB agents I made fun of in Stockholm.

My job is done. Vanya is on U.S. soil with all the paperwork he'll need in Detroit for now. If anything else comes up, the Chargers will take care of it.

This is where we part ways. Vanya and the Americans will drive to Detroit from here and I have to catch a train to Brooklyn. My uncle and I have business to discuss in Brighton Beach.

"Thank you for all of your help and planning," Chris Brookins tells me as we shake hands.

I smile. "Always happy to help a comrade escape the regime."

After shaking hands with Brookins' Detroit sidekick, I turn to my friend. "If you need me, never hesitate to call."

"Thank you," Vanya says. "For everything."

"It's my pleasure to help, brother." When he brings me in for a hug, I slap his back. "We will meet again."

Before he lets me go, he whispers, "I have a lump in my stomach, Kirya. Promise me you'll take care of Stasya."

"Don't worry. I always have, and I always will," I give him my word as I back away.

3

STASYA

Moscow

"*Y*our brother is gone," Papa says in greeting as I enter our room after work. He's sitting at the table, pouring himself a glass of vodka.

I tilt my head, confused. "Well, of course he is, Papa. He's in Sweden for the World Tournament."

He downs his drink and slams the glass on the table, which shakes the plates and silverware *Babushka* set for dinner. "He is not in Stockholm, Anastasiya. He is in America. Defected."

"They're calling him a deserter," *Babushka* says from behind me. She edges past and places a large bowl of potatoes on the table.

"He *is* a deserter," Papa reminds her. "No matter how happy we are for him, he is still a criminal."

"He went to America," I whisper. While Papa sits there, drinking to Vanya's escape, realization of what he's said makes me lightheaded, and I think I may faint.

"Come, Stasya." *Babushka* waves me toward her. "Help me bring the rest of the food in."

I follow her down the hallway to the kitchen, numb to feeling, oblivious to the bustling of multiple families cooking at the same time. I duck under the wet clothes hanging on the one of the clotheslines that runs through the kitchen, and allow *Babushka* to fill my hands with plates.

Not even the enticing smell of cabbage rolls snaps me out of my funk.

My twin brother left for America without me. How could he? After all of our promises? Just over a month ago, before he left for this trip, he stood on the metro platform, hugging me, and telling me he'd take me with him if he ever left.

After we've brought all the food to our room, my grandmother and I join Papa.

"We're getting closer and closer to freedom," he says sarcastically before scooping a heaping forkful into his mouth. "Maybe Vanya will send us money. We could become business owners. What kind of business shall we open?"

"I'd rather have Vanya than his money," I say, pushing boiled potatoes around my plate, wishing I were with my brother—or that he were here and everything was like old times. Not that I wish it on him, to be here instead of living his dream in America, but the sadness of losing him is draining me, mentally and emotionally.

"Things are changing, little bird. And who knows what will happen to us now," *Babushka* says uncharacteristically. She doesn't usually say much about the changes in the country, unless she's offering us glimpses of her youth.

"What does that mean?" I ask.

"While you were at work, the KGB was here, banging on the door, demanding answers about your brother—your *twin*—

36

who left us behind for money and freedom. They think I knew. 'How could a son not talk to his father about such an important life decision,' they asked?" The contempt in Papa's voice is crystal clear. He's hurt and angry at Vanya.

I watch him toss back two more glasses of vodka. "Everything is changing. Everything you know today will be different tomorrow."

"It takes longer than one day for everything to change." I brush his comments off.

"Did you know, Stasya?" my grandmother asks quietly, lifting her eyes from her plate.

"Did I know what?"

"Don't be stupid!" Papa barks.

Babushka shoots him a dirty look, but her voice is calm when she clarifies her question. "Did you know Vanya was leaving?"

They're both staring, waiting for my answer. It's as if time has stopped.

"I did not," I tell them, avoiding their eyes. No matter what I say, they'll think I'm lying. Vanya and I are far too close for them to believe I didn't know—even if it's the truth.

Papa's dark, bushy eyebrows narrow as he glares at me. "It's hard to believe, you know," he says in an accusatory tone. "You and your brother share everything."

"Ever since the womb, yes, I know." I set my fork down and place my fists on the table, before taking a deep breath. "Of course, we talked about how excited he was at being drafted by Detroit, but he never once mentioned defecting."

"America has stolen my son, the only one who brought joy to this family," Papa muses, shaking the vodka bottle to get the last drops into his glass.

"He won't forget us, Papa." I assure him quietly. I'm used to the stabbing comments. Vanya has always had a higher place in Papa's heart. He is my father's only son. Playing for the CSA team brought pride to our family and Mother Russia. "He'll contact us when he's able."

"Contact us? Why would he do that? He has money and fame. He doesn't need us—not even you. He left like a coward in the night." The dark circles under Papa's eyes are so pronounced, it looks like someone painted grayish-purple crescents there. "You think I couldn't hear you two talking at night? You think I didn't know about your plans to go to America with him to get away from me?"

He shoves his plate at me angrily, sending potatoes and cabbage onto my lap. When he grabs a bowl and cocks his arm back, I jump up and raise my hands to shield the attack.

"Misha!" *Babushka* cries out.

"The joke is on you, isn't it, Anastasiya?" he mocks, lowering the bowl as he watches me brush the food from my thighs onto the floor. "How does it feel to be left behind? To be left in a country crumbling more every day while your brother enjoys freedom in *America*."

Tears spring to my eyes. Being hit or beaten hurts when it happens, but physical pain eases. The mental and emotional damage he's caused has warped my mind in ways I'll never be able to measure. Papa knows exactly what to say to cause the most pain. The things that penetrate like a hammer through my heart.

"Be sure to keep your emotions in check when the KGB comes for you," Papa warns, grabbing the empty bottle of vodka. "They won't be swayed by glassy eyes and a trembling lip when it comes to your brother's desertion."

My stomach tightens and I clench my teeth, bracing myself

for the worst, but instead of throwing it at me, he leans down and sets the empty container on the floor.

"Why don't you make yourself useful and get me another bottle?" he sneers, relishing in the knowledge of how much he scares me.

Rather than answer, I rush past him and out the door. Once I'm in the hallway, I don't stop against the wall and slide to the floor like I did when I was a girl.

No.

This time, I keep running.

4

KIRYA

The first time I rode the Q Train to the Brighton Beach area of Brooklyn, I was nervous about missing the stop. All my worries subsided while looking out the window. Familiar Cyrillic letters are everywhere. Signage for stores and restaurants are all in Russian and English. Though nicknamed "Little Odessa" because of the Russian and Ukrainian immigrants who settled in this area, there's no resemblance to Odessa—or even Moscow, for that matter. It looks like Brooklyn's been translated into Russian. It feels like home, but not.

Exhausted from the constant adrenaline over the last few days, I grab a coffee to keep myself awake. I feel like a feral cat who got the shit beat out of him and dragged through an alley. And if I look half as exhausted as I feel, my mother will freak the fuck out.

Plus, I need my wits about me when I'm with my uncle. He

may be like a father to me, but he's still the leader of Russian organized crime in North America.

The walk to Brighton Peaks, the oceanfront complex where my uncle and mother share a luxury apartment, takes less than five minutes. The boring faded, brick high-rise looming over the Brighton Beach boardwalk with ornate, white balconies jutting out of each floor couldn't be more different than his home in Moscow.

After I graduated from university, my uncle let me move into his four-room apartment on Gorky Street. It's located on the top floor of a beautiful building designed by Arkady Mordvinov in the 1940s in the Stalinist Empire style. Sure, the Peaks' proximity to the ocean is a bonus, but if I want to live in an ugly brick box, I can do that in Moscow.

I wade through puddles on Brighton Beach Avenue before making a right at the corner with the Brooklyn Public Library. My head pounds and my nose starts to run, a telltale sign of Spring in New York. Flowers are blooming and trees are spewing shit I'm not used to inhaling.

It's a reminder of how different it is from Moscow. Here, I worry about puddles from rainfall and melted snowbanks and plants that wreak havoc on my allergies. In Moscow, I'm less worried about that than the dead bodies that appear when the snow thaws.

I enter the building and take the elevator the thirteenth floor. I rap on the door three times, draining my coffee as I wait for someone to answer.

My mother whips the door open, greeting me with tears in her eyes. She looks more vibrant and beautiful than I ever remember. Healthy, blonde hair bounces above her shoulders and her once hollow cheeks are plump, with a natural, rosy glow. Though I miss her dearly, choosing to live here with my uncle, soaking up the sunshine and freedom, is the best decision she ever made.

I step inside and pull her into my arms.

"Kirya! My Kirya! You're finally here," she says, squeezing me as hard as she can. At barely over five feet tall, she's not a big woman, but she's sturdy and strong. Her embrace feels like it could crack my ribs.

"What is this 'finally'?" I ask with a laugh. "It's only been a few months since I was last here."

"I'm allowed to miss my son," she says, pinching the top of my ear. I bat at her hand.

My uncle strolls up behind Mama, greeting me with a cigarette hanging from his upturned lips. He plucks it from his mouth, letting out a stream of smoke into my face. I cough as I waving the cloud away. He's always got a way to remind me who's boss.

"Kirya!" He wags his curled fingers, beckoning me to come further inside. "Come in. Come in. "

"Good to see you, Uncle Vitya!" I step into the large living room and kiss his cheeks before giving him a quick hug.

After ten years in America, Viktor is almost unrecognizable. When he left Moscow, he was as thin as the cigarette between his fingers. His rotund belly and chubby, red cheeks are a telltale sign of a life of excess. Still, even with extra weight and gray stubble dusting his jaw and upper lip, he looks younger than he did twenty years ago.

Maybe Americans get their water from the fountain of youth. The only thing left from his harder days are his crooked, yellow teeth.

"Good flight?" he asks, closing the door behind me and taking the duffle bag out of my hands.

I nod.

"Are you hungry?" Mama asks. "You must be, after a flight all the way from Sweden," she continues before I have a chance to answer. "I'll make you a snack."

"Not too much!" Viktor tells her. "I'm taking him to see the restaurant today."

"Then I should make him double! Not even a dog should eat the food at that place," she mutters.

"What restaurant?" I ask, following him through a small, but extravagant living room.

If anyone ever doubted my uncle's wealth, all they'd have to do is look at his apartment. Everything is antique and overly ornate. From the frames on the artwork to the beautiful Oriental rugs covering the gorgeous hardwood floors. It's the same way in his Moscow residence, though there, the Oriental rugs hang on the walls like tapestries.

He looks over his shoulder and winks at me. "I bought you a present."

When we reach his office, he nods at the brown leather wingback chair across from his mahogany desk as he stomps his cigarette out in a brass ashtray.

"You bought me a restaurant?" I ask, lowering myself into the chair. The tension leaves my shoulders as I sink into the back, letting the wings envelope me, relaxing for the first time since I left Sweden. There's still a massive pain surging in my head, but I'll grab some medicine to take care of that.

He sets the duffel bag down and riffles through it, stopping when he finds the bulging envelope he's looking for. "You look like shit," he says, pushing the bag to the ground. Good thing I didn't pack anything breakable.

"I feel even worse." I lean forward, resting my elbows on my knees and rubbing my forehead. "Fuck spring in New York."

Viktor laughs. "It was bad for me at first too. Go to the *banya* tomorrow. Dry that shit up."

"There's nothing I'd love more than to relax in a steam bath right now, but there's no time. My flight to Moscow is at six a.m."

"Your mother's going to be pissed." He looks up from the stack of cash he's counting. "She's been waiting for you."

"She knew this wasn't a social visit."

It's harsh but true. I love my mother with all my heart, and I know she's safe here with Viktor. Maybe someday I'll be in the United States full-time. Until then, I'm happy I get to see her a few times a year, even if the visits are short.

"You're so much like me, I could be looking in a mirror."

"Dear god, I hope not!" I pat the top of my head and run my fingers through my hair to make sure it's still there, teasing my uncle about his balding dome.

"You're a funny man today, yes?" Viktor says dryly.

I just smile and settle back into the seat, stretching my legs out and crossing them at the ankles. The old, worn leather is soft and welcoming, I could easily fall asleep right here.

"There is a lot of money to be made right now, Kirya," he says. His hazel eyes glow green, the shade of the American dollars stacked in front of him. "You getting Kravtsov to Detroit is just the beginning."

"Is that how we're going to capitalize?" I ask. "I'll be going back and forth, helping Russians defect?"

He shakes his head. "No. Not for long, at least." He shoves his chair away from the table, puts his feet up, and lights another cigarette. "There won't be many more athletes defecting. There's too much money to be made on them. You think Sovietsport is going to let that go?"

Sovietsport is a State-run group of companies responsible

for importing and exporting sporting equipment, negotiating sponsorships, and sending athletes to other countries. Soviet athletes are in demand—and the government knows it.

"No, but I don't think they'll give up their most prized work-horses either. What's the catch?"

"Money. Money is always the catch," Viktor says. "The state is strapped and they need to do something. They are selling players to the NHL."

"Really?" I lean forward, interested in the new development. A few of the older guys on the Scarlet Army team have been to begging to be allowed to go to the NHL for years.

"If a player has been drafted, they are going to let him go to America"—he waves his cigarette around as he speaks—"or Canada. But the player will not get his full salary, you see. Sovietsport will draw eighty percent of it."

"Eighty percent?" I laugh. "Who would agree to that?"

My uncle's smile disappears. "Who wouldn't, Kirya? You know how they live. Eleven months at that dilapidated training base in the middle of nowhere." His face is stone-cold sober. "They can't even get their dicks sucked. Not even the married ones."

I nod, understanding why a player would go, even for such a shitty financial deal. They play in tournaments all over Europe and North America and see the freedom—the opportunity. They will do anything to get to the West. Twenty percent of a five hundred-thousand-dollar contract is still more than they will ever make back home.

"So how does this benefit us?" I ask. Time to get to the point. And there must be a point if my uncle brought me in to discuss this opportunity. "If the money is going to Sovietsport, what sense is it to help them?"

"Well, it is always good sense to help—influence—those in

power, yes?" His eyebrows raise with his hypothetical question. "It will not go through the sports committee for long, my boy." He pauses and smiles. "Soon, there will be no Soviet Union. And when that happens, players will be free to go without paying anyone. The Americans and Canadians, they are not stupid. They know Soviet players will flee in droves."

"And we will be there to assist them," I finish the thought.

"Exactly." Viktor takes another drag on the cigarette and slowly lets out the smoke. "By helping Kravtsov, you have gained a reputation, Kirya. Players trust him and he will recommend you."

Vanya will recommend me even if he doesn't want to. That's part of our agreement.

"I can also approach them too, yes?"

"I expect you to. I can get you a list of players who have already been drafted by NHL teams. You will contact them in the order of who was drafted highest. Because those are the players they want the most. The ones they will pay big dollars too. You know the talent here, Kirya. Hockey is in your blood."

He's right. I grew up playing hockey with Vanya. But unlike him, when the Scarlet Army selected me for the junior team, I refused. I was making too much money selling the things I bought off foreigners. Thanks to my uncle's guidance, I was already living the life I wanted to live. Money over hockey wasn't a difficult decision for me, and going back to being under strict Soviet rules and discipline wasn't even an option.

"I should also go after the new kids, the ones coming up in the system," I say, already mulling over ideas. The opportunity to represent Russian hockey players in North America is exciting. It's also an easy sell, since they'll need someone to help translate and negotiate their contracts. Who better than me—someone who understands hockey, business, and the language.

"You must focus on the best ones, Kirya. Get to them before someone decides to do the same thing. If you have a relationship established, it will be harder for others to squeeze in."

"Well, I'm sure you have a plan for the people who try to poach our players anyway."

Viktor laughs. "I'm trying to get you away from that, my boy."

"It's hard when I'm in charge of collections at the market, Vitya. If something has to be taken care of, I do it."

"Yes, I know. You take after me." He looks up at me as he extinguishes his cigarette. "But I'd still rather you let Slava and Igor do that part. Keep your hands relatively clean for now." He continues, "You know how different the media is in America. They aren't spewing government propaganda. They have freedom to write whatever they want. And Soviet hockey players leaving is international news."

I nod. While in America, I witnessed the media's bloodlust for a story firsthand. I'm still surprised Vanya made it to Detroit. Reporters tracked his every move on TV and in the newspapers. They were even at the airport when he arrived, with cameras and video recorders catching every move. There was a press conference about the ordeal the next day. It was an absolute circus.

My uncle has been one step ahead of the curve his entire life. He's got a brilliant mind, hundreds of relationships and agreements with members of the highest levels of Soviet government, and zero morals. All of which explain how he's risen so high in organized crime.

At five years old, he set me up with a personal English tutor. When I complained, he told me it was one of the most important languages I could ever learn. Despite my initial hesitance, I speak the language almost as well as a native. My studies served me well as a young entrepreneur, trading Russian things for American goods. Being able to converse gave me the upper hand over other kids trying to do the same thing. It's a lot easier to trust a Russian who speaks the English language than one throwing out random words and phrases.

"They'll link me to you," I tell my uncle. "There's no doubt about that."

"Yes. That's why when I say Slava and Igor will handle things like collections, you will listen, you understand?"

I nod again. As an *Avtoritet,* or "authority" in the Bratva, I may be a high-ranking soldier, but I'm still a soldier.

"How will we get paid?" I ask.

"Legally," Viktor answers. "You remember that business I started with Vashnikov?"

I nod.

A year ago, my uncle opened a sports and entertainment company, with Sergei Vashnikov. A few days later, a sniper gunned down Vashnikov as he left a bathhouse. And just like that, Viktor become the only owner.

People like my uncle have seen the end of the Soviet Union coming. While many citizens live in fear, we're counting down the days. Once the country breaks apart, those of us who formed relationships in the West and started businesses here early will become even richer.

"I've split the companies into two. From this moment on, you are the owner and CEO of New World Management. Being a sports agent is a perfectly legal career all over the world. You negotiate contracts and communication between the players and organizations and you get paid. *We* get paid."

"Eighty percent?" I smirk, though I'm enamored at Viktor's ability to think ahead again. Someday, I hope to have the same strategic brilliance.

"No. But it will be enough. An old friend is drawing up contract documents now. A lawyer I know from the zone."

"A lawyer you know from prison?" I ask. "That's who I'm trusting to come up with legal and legitimate contracts?"

"He wasn't in prison *with* me, Kirya." Viktor laughs again. "He helped many of us get out."

For someone who's killed more people than I can count, my uncle seems as normal as any man walking down the street. Once his clothes are off, the tattoos adorning his body tell the story of who he is: *vory v zakone*, a professional criminal with a high-level position in organized crime and authority over lower-level members.

He follows a strict code, which, among other things, says he's never to marry or have children. But family is extremely important to him. I'm sure that's the reason he's always doted on my mother and me, providing us everything we needed and anything we wanted, even after he moved to the United States.

Which is why I'm slightly surprised he's offering me legitimate work. His code also states he's never to participate in legal work, but live only on what he's gained through criminal means.

"Please excuse me, Uncle. I don't mean to offend you with this question, but this seems out of character," I begin cautiously. "Doesn't this business directly violate your rules?"

Viktor explained the *vory* code to me when I started working with him as a teenager. Since I've never been to prison, I can't claim the title. It's a generation of criminals that has impressive power now—especially with their influence on government officials, but they're losing steam to the new gangsters, the ones who don't follow any code at all. Rising up in organized crime under his wing means I've had his protection and his power. Though I earned my position, I can't deny I've had opportunities because of him.

"I'm no longer attached to the business, Kirya. It will be yours and you are not *vory*."

After all these years, he is still providing for me. The father I never had.

He has given his family the best life we could possibly have, while still keeping us under the radar to the criminal activity he's involved in and the company he keeps. We lived in communal housing assigned by my mother's employer, but we had access to things no one else in our apartment could get.

When my grandparents got tired of living in the city, he moved them into an enormous *dacha* 130 kilometers northwest of Moscow. It was a beautiful two-story house with marble floors and columns. Not long after, I left the apartment to go to university, leaving my mother in a room that was once shared by four of us. For a few years, she felt like a queen.

"What if they don't accept my services?" I ask.

"Don't worry about that. We have hundreds of Slavas and Igors we can send to change their mind."

Viktor and I discuss the plan for my new business venture for another half hour, before he stops abruptly and jumps out of his chair. "The restaurant!"

I lean back stunned at the sudden change of direction.

"We must go now," he says, opening the top drawer of his desk and grabbing a gun. He walks to the door, stuffing it into his waistband. "Kiss your mother."

I kiss my mother goodbye, and follow Viktor to the elevator. "You will love this place, Kirya. When I saw it for sale, I knew you had to have it."

It only takes a moment for my uncle to hail a cab, and we're on our way, weaving through the crowded streets of Manhattan.

As we approach the restaurant my uncle bought me, excitement builds like a balloon, getting bigger and bigger as we get closer.

But as soon as we step inside, it deflates.

I spin around, taking in the bland, outdated décor and dilapidated furniture. Everything looks like it's covered with a layer of dirt bleach won't even wipe away. I can't believe this restaurant hasn't been shut down by the health department. "This place needs a lot of work."

"I have faith that you can bring it back to its glory, Kirya." He shoves a photo album into my chest. The cover is a deep red with *The Russian Dining Room* in scrolling gold script.

My jaw drops as I flip through the pages. Inside, photos capture a formerly breathtaking space, whimsical and bold, highlighting the excess and grandeur of Imperial Russia. It's a complete one eighty from the boring, bland room surrounding us. It looks as if someone came through and stole every piece of rich Russian character. "This doesn't even look like the same place. What happened to it?"

"It fell on hard times over the last few years. Someone bought it and did this." He spits on the floor. "I believe their mission was to change it completely. But I couldn't have them get rid of a historic gem like this, could I? When their financing fell through, I scooped it up."

"We need a beautiful space like this to gather in the city. Think of the parties we can hold here."

Despite having the historical proof in my hands, it's hard to imagine this was ever a place people wanted to gather.

I toss the album on to the bar. "I'm not a designer."

"True, but I know you appreciate a challenge. You're smart enough to figure out how to bring it back. You have the kind of mind that can merge the most interesting parts of Russian culture and cuisine into a profitable restaurant. It'll be a sparkling gem again."

"I appreciate the confidence."

"Plus, it's another way to get you to New York."

"You really want me here?"

"Want is not the right word, Kirya. I need you here."

"I have business in Moscow."

"You will phase that out over the next year while you are recruiting clients," he tells me. Then he walks toward the door. "Come on. Your mother's cursing us right now."

I nod and follow him through the front door to West 57th Street. "When I was a boy, if you would have told me I was going to be a sports agent and a restaurateur in New York City, I would have laughed at you."

"Why? I always told you that you could be anything you wanted to be."

"I wanted to be like you."

"Don't strive for that, Kirya! You are a much, much better human than I will ever be."

The entire course of my life changed in the last twenty-four hours. I never saw a future outside of organized crime—didn't care about that kind of future unless I had freedom. Now, I'm the owner of two legit businesses. I've never been so excited to get back to Moscow so I can prepare to leave for good.

* * *

When we get back to Viktor's apartment in Brighton Beach, Mama tells me I have an urgent message from Slava.

When I call back, he answers immediately despite the six-hour time difference.

"What's wrong?" I ask without greeting.

"Kravtsov's defection is big news, Kirya," he says. "KGB is watching the family already. And Igor overheard one of Sobakin's goons today at the market, talking about taking the sister."

Fuck!

"I have the first flight out tomorrow morning. Have Igor get some guys to watch Sobakin's men and Kravtsov's family. But I want you on the sister, Slava. Don't let her out of your sight."

"What about KGB?"

"Fuck those pussies!"

KGB is annoying, but not an organization I fear anymore. My main concern is Stasya. Before we parted ways at JFK Airport yesterday, I made Vanya a promise and I intend to keep it.

5

STASYA

*T*he Central Scarlet Army's training *baza* is in the middle of nowhere. I'm not supposed to know where it is—not even player's wives are supposed to know—but Vanya called me once after a particularly strenuous workout. He said he was worried that he'd die out there and he wanted someone to be able to find him.

It's early afternoon when I reach the base. I left work after lunch because I wasn't exactly sure how long it would take me to get there after I got off the metro. It ended up being a kilometer walk, then another half-kilometer up a long, grassy road to the complex. My feet hurt and I'm completely out of breath when I reach the gate.

"I need to speak to Lieutenant Morozov," I tell the guard. "It's an emergency."

"Emergency? What kind of emergency?" he asks. His dark

eyes assess me under his military cap. A red Soviet star with a yellow hammer and sickle in the middle sparkles like a gem.

I bite my tongue. I can't divulge that I came to ask Dima about Vanya or I'll be hauled off for questioning.

"It's a personal matter," I say quietly, keeping my eyes locked on nothing in particular over his shoulder, averting his gaze. Slowly, I bring my hands to my belly and cradle it.

His eyebrows furrow as he shifts his gaze from my face to my stomach. Then, as if a lightbulb goes off, he grunts and nods. "I'll get him."

If there's a law about lying to an officer, I'm definitely getting locked up. But I couldn't care less at this point. Life in Russia without my brother is a jail sentence anyway.

A few minutes later, I hear Dima's footsteps coming fast and loud as he runs toward the gate. "Anastasiya!" he calls out. He's breathing hard when he gets to me. "What's going on? Peshkov said you're—"

"Dima! What happened? Where's Vanya?" I ask desperately.

"Shhh! Keep your voice down, Stasya!" He glances over his shoulder as if he's being followed, but the guard is nowhere in sight. "What are you doing here? Peshkov said you're pregnant."

"What else could I say that would allow him to let you out here to talk to me?"

A wave of relief crosses his face, but then he seems worried again. "You can't be here, Stasya. It's not safe. They're questioning everyone." His eyes implore me to leave, but I can't—I won't—until I find out what he knows about my brother.

"Everyone is so worried about my safety—and I'm worried about Vanya. What happened?" I plead. "Where is he?"

"He's gone!" Dima says harshly.

"Did you know?" I ask again, balling my fists at my side as I fight back the tears. My voice gets higher, sorrow filling every word. "When we were all waiting for the train, talking like it was any other day, did you know that I'd never see my brother again?"

"You being here is dangerous, Anastasiya!" he pleads with me. "Not just for you—but all of us." He presses a finger to his lips and tilts his head, as if listening for something or someone. "If they see me talking to you—" He trails off.

"How can you be so cold?" I ask, grief cracking my voice. Rage pumps adrenaline through my veins and I pound on his chest until I collapse against him, my forehead falling onto the silver zipper of his red training jacket.

"Take your hands off me this minute." He grabs my wrists and pushes me from his chest. "Vanya is a traitor to his country. I have nothing else to say about the deserter. Now please leave the premises before you are escorted away," he says through clenched teeth.

A large, uniformed man hurries toward Dima and I. "Who are you? What are you doing here?"

"I'm sorry to bother you, *Lieutenant*," I mock Dima.

Swallowing back anger and tears, I spin around and run as fast as I can. My heart pounds, pumping anger through my veins. Once I've made it to the end of the grassy road, I stop, bend over, and place my hands on my knees. My entire body shakes, and I finally let the tears I've been holding in flow.

Dmitri Morozov is dead to me.

Considering our history, it should be an easy decision to make, but today's interaction sealed my hatred.

When I reach the Metro, I rush down the stairs with tears still streaming down my face. The platform is so congested, I have to elbow my way through the doors. There will be another one in a few minutes, but it's Friday night and waiting won't make a difference. Either way, I'll be fighting the crowd; the people wearing drab, gray work clothes, on their way home for the day, or those with slight pops of color, dressed up to go out for the evening.

Maybe that's what *I* should do. When I get home, I should get dressed up, call Svetlana, and ask her to meet me at the discotheque. Maybe letting loose to Victor Tsoi's latest song is just what I need to help me drown away the pain of Dima's cold indifference when I asked him if he knew about my brother's defection to America.

The train jolts abruptly before heaving forward as it leaves the station. I plant my feet firmly for balance and tighten my grip on the bar overhead.

I haven't stopped crying since I left the Central Scarlet Army's hockey training base. Thankfully, anyone who's glanced my way has quickly averted their gaze. I close my eyes and take a deep breath, wiping away tears with the back of my free hand.

All I wanted was some answers. My twin brother, Vanya, who has shared everything with me since the womb, defected to the United States after a tournament in Sweden. Despite us being so close, he never uttered one word about it before he left. I thought going to Dima, his best friend on the team, would help me understand how my brother could have kept such a huge secret from me.

But the arrogant coward refused to reveal what he knew.

They were roommates. Friends! Was he not concerned or— at the very least—*inquisitive* when Vanya packed his bags and left?

Dima said he's scared. *He's* scared.

My family is being treated like criminals—being followed and questioned by the KGB—because of Vanya's desertion, and *Dima* is scared.

To be afraid is normal, but when a lieutenant in the military is a coward? That's unacceptable. Those in a position of power who have the ability to help must rise up. Though there may have been a time when I had feelings for him, I have no use for a chicken like him in my life.

When the train stops at *Aviamotornaya* station, I feel so numb and disoriented, it's as if the crowd is carrying me out the doors and up the stairs. I've walked home from here so many times, I do it on autopilot.

Vanya used to scold me for walking alone because the streets have gotten colder and darker over the last few years. He wasn't concerned about the weather or season, but the criminals and the violence they bring.

Mafia is everywhere, but I'm not scared. Gangs kill for money, power, and greed. They want something that someone else has.

I have nothing.

Besides, the *Bratva* is the least of my concerns. I have more to fear right in my own home. Ever since Mama died, I've become the lone target of my father's anger and violence.

Vanya's hockey accomplishments were the only bright moments in our mundane conversations. Now, we have nothing —just the bleak reality that he left us all behind.

For years, my brother swore he'd take me with him if he ever got the chance to live in America. He promised me again just a few weeks ago, minutes before he left for his most recent hockey tournament.

And now he's gone. And I'm here, stuck amid chaos and instability unlike anything I've ever lived through before in Russia.

At least life under communism was stable—boring, but stable.

The KGB has already harassed Papa, *Babushka*, and half of

the other families who live in our apartment, asking them what they knew about Vanya's defection. It's only a matter of time before they come for me.

The thought of a KGB interrogation makes my stomach lurch. Though I rarely drink, I may join my father at the table with a glass of vodka tonight. I need something to numb the anger, betrayal, and heartbreak stewing for Vanya.

The concentrated gasoline smell permeates the air. I've gotten so used to the influx of vehicles taking to the roads over the last few years, I don't usually notice. But today, anxiety has my sensitive stomach bubbling with every inhale.

I've just crossed *Aviamotornaya Ulitsa* when, out of the corner of my eye, I notice a rusty Vaz creeping up the street. My jaw twitches involuntarily. Feeling a bit stupid for being nervous of an old car, I nuzzle my chin into my scarf and keep my gaze forward until it passes.

The loud rev of an engine makes me jump, and a shiny, black sedan speeds past and screeches to a stop a few meters ahead of me. My legs shake and I stumble over an uneven crack in the sidewalk.

Vaz is a common brand here, but black BMWs are only driven by mafia. Being stuck in the middle of crossfire between two gangs was not how I expected the day to end. But it's also not a surprise considering how the rest of it has gone.

I hold my breath, watching intensely as the sedan's driver and passenger doors fling open at the same time. Two men covered in black head-to-toe jump out and sprint toward me. My heart thumps in beat with their heavy footsteps pounding the concrete, each step getting louder as they get closer.

Swallowing back fear, I increase my speed and move to the side, giving the men space to get wherever they're going.

Suddenly, the taller of the two clasps his thick arms around me and starts carrying me toward the car. The other crouches down, grabs the bag I dropped, and sprints to the driver's side.

"No!" I scream as I kick my feet and fight to free myself. "Stop!"

It's a futile effort. There's no one on the road other than the Vaz, and the people inside know better than to try to stop mafia.

I stretch my legs to the ground, dragging my feet in an attempt to slow him down, but instead of having any effect, my shoes scrape against the sidewalk and one falls off. He tightens his grip and lifts me into the air.

When we get to the car, he yanks the door open and shoves me in face-first before slamming the door shut. It jars my feet, propelling my body forward and sending my cheek sliding across the seat.

"Please!" I cry out. "Please don't do this!" My clammy palms slip on the leather as I try to claw myself upright.

Instead of responding, the passenger spins around and leans forward. Cold sweat beads on my forehead as I scramble backward, pressing my spine against the seat. He wedges himself between the two front seats, grabs a fistful of hair, and pulls me toward him. I shake my head violently, but his grip doesn't loosen, and my jerky movements only enhance the pain.

He deftly wraps rope around my wrists, pulling it tight before making a complicated knot. When he's finished, he looks up. Icy blue eyes peer at me through the opening of the black balaclava masking his face.

When I gasp, he slams a foul-smelling rag against my mouth and I involuntarily ingest whatever's on the cloth. Only one thought runs through my head before everything goes black.

I know those eyes.

6

STASYA

*D*espite there being no light in the room, it burns to open my eyes. Blinking isn't any better. My head pounds. My throat stings. My eyelids flutter shut.

The next time I wake up, my head still hurts, but at least I can keep my eyes open. I lift my cheek from the freezing floor and struggle to sit up. I'd started to wake from the effects of whatever drug was on the rag they stuffed in my mouth when the tall man shoved me into the room. Then, I slipped and fell face-first. Because my hands are tied, I couldn't properly brace the fall. Bashing my head on the floor is the last thing I remember.

Maybe it wasn't mafia, as I originally thought. Maybe it's KGB, taking me in for questioning about Vanya's defection. But why would they be wearing masks? KGB don't have to hide. They think it's within their authority to haul people away, no face protection necessary.

I touch my forehead and a jolt of pain sears through me. There's no blood on my fingers, but I feel like there has to be a gash. Maybe it's dried, because it hurts too damn bad to be bruised.

One side of my body doesn't seem to work, numb from lying on the cold concrete. I rub my hands together, trying to warm them up. The sting feels like pins and needles as circulation comes back.

Suddenly, the door opens and prickly goose bumps pop up along my arms. The thought of being questioned by KGB already had me nervous, now I'm terrified.

I squint at the figure, trying to make out features to remember if I ever get out of here alive, but all I can see is a dark orb surrounded by a halo of bright light from the hallway.

As the door closes, my eyes adjust and my heart soars.

"Kirya!" I croak in surprise. My eyes well up with tears, seeing the familiar face of my old friend. Despite the joy, my heart pumps faster, a mixture of excitement and fear, as I frantically scan the room for the man who dropped me in here. "Help me, Kirya!" I whisper loudly, rising to my knees and shaking my bound hands in a silent plea. "Hurry! Before he comes back."

"Too late," he whispers, tucking his black hair behind one ear, revealing his face. He's just as handsome as I remember. A five o'clock shadow dusts his strong jaw and chiseled cheekbones. My eyes go straight to his full, pink lips as they have since I was thirteen. I've never seen his hair so long. It falls past his ears and brushes the middle of his neck.

His appearance wasn't the only reason Kirya became the first boy I had a crush on, but seeing him standing here, looking so handsome, reminds me why he had such a huge effect on my teenage years.

The initial excitement at seeing him drains, along with any hope in my heart. Despite the memories, I swallow hard before looking at him again. Glaring back at me are the same eyes I saw before I passed out, cold and hard as ice. "You are him."

"Yes, Stasya. I am him," he affirms, using the familiar diminutive of my name, as if we met on the street, and he didn't kidnap me and dump me in a damp room. His long, black, leather trench coat flaps against his calves as he stalks closer. A glint of silver flashes at his side.

I close my eyes and fall back on my calves, defeated.

The man standing before me with sinister, hooded eyes and a knife clutched in his hand is not the sweet boy I grew up with. He is not the boy who would slide to the floor, put a comforting arm around me, and sit next to me in the shared hallway between our family's rooms after Papa hit me.

Kirya must have heard the yelling and slamming—maybe even the beating itself—as the walls we shared were very thin. There are no secrets in communal living.

Everyone in the apartment knew what was going on, as we'd seen it many times within the families over the years. And it wasn't just men; I'd seen Maria Borisovich beat her husband with a bag of potatoes. For as much as everyone is in each other's business, living in the same spaces and sharing everything, no one talked about the violence. It's so common, no one blinks an eye. There were even jokes. *"Misha is drunk again. Stasya better hide the frying pans!"*

What could I do? Walk away from my father? Leave my family? Where would I go? It's so common that no one even batted an eye.

Except Kirya.

He'd do anything to cheer me up—ridiculous jokes, sharing his grand plans for the future, sometimes give me treats, like candy or special fruit. I remember the first time he shared a banana with me. Despite my appreciation, I couldn't help the look of disgust that crossed my face when he brought out the odd-looking fruit and started peeling back the yellow skin. Then he offered me a piece and urged me to try it. It was so sweet and delicious I almost cried. There were no exotic fruits at the store where we shopped.

Kirya's uncle must have been a high-ranking official because he brought them treats whenever he came for dinner. At the time, I thought that was the only way they could have gotten such special things.

The curve of the blade in his hand reminds me of that silly banana—a resemblance that brings me back to the present situation. And now I understand.

The only people who wear black leather coats in today's turbulent times are mafia.

The man standing inches away, looking down on me as though I were just another stain on this dirty floor, is not that same man I thought I'd fallen in love with during the years he protected me from Papa's abuse when my brother wasn't around.

This Kirya is the man who got so upset, he beat my father to within an inch of his life the last night I saw him.

The sliver of light from the cracked door seems as bright as the afternoon sun after being stuck this pitch-black room with no windows. I squint, trying to remember his cold, hard eyes as I once knew them. Back when the light blue hue resembled that of dreams and clouds—things that could carry me away from my miserable existence.

"Why have you done this?" I ask meekly.

Kirya pauses, looking at me pensively before answering. "Short answer: You belong to me now. Long answer: I saved your life."

"Excuse me?" I ask, blinking a few times to make sure I'm

awake and not in a bizarre nightmare, gaining my voice in the process. "How do I *belong* to you?"

"I won you in a card game." He shakes his head dismissively, as if that's the end of the subject. "It was a long time ago."

"You won me in a card game," I repeat. "What the hell does that mean? 'You won me.' I'm not a piece of property."

"That's true, but your father keeps gambling with no means to pay. He said he had nothing of value, but I begged to differ." His lips turn up in a smile, but it's not kind or friendly. It's the sinister smile of someone toying with me.

"I'm not my father's property," I say, ignoring his back-handed compliment.

How can I stop to appreciate anything when my life is worth so little that my father offered it up in a card game?

"You're free to walk out right now." He gestures toward the door. Silky, black hair pops out from where he'd tucked it behind his ear.

"Are you serious?" I ask. After being thrown onto a filthy, freezing floor in a dark room and left for hours, I can't help but be suspicious. But I'm also intrigued to find out why he'd offer to let me leave. My gaze shifts from the door to him. "What's the catch?"

"It's not a catch, but there is something."

"Of course there is." I roll my eyes. He's mafia. There's always a catch.

"But it's still your choice, Stasya. I'll give you the facts—and the offer—and you can decide."

Any hope I had of returning home, to the warmth and stability of my apartment, seeps out in a slow, sad breath.

A mafia thug would never give me an offer or choice that benefits me. Not even a thug I once loved.

Kirya raises the knife and I recoil immediately. He smirks,

amused by my fear. Instead of striking me, he saws the rope at my wrists, freeing me within seconds. I flex my hands a few times, working out the tightness from being bound for hours.

"Thank you," I say quietly, figuring it can't hurt to use manners when being held against my will.

"I'll admit these aren't the nicest accommodations." Kirya looks around the dank room. "But I saved you from being kidnapped, so I figured it would be okay for a few hours."

The irony isn't lost on me. "You kidnapped me to save me from being kidnapped?" I ask, slowly getting to my feet on legs that feel too soft and wobbly to support my weight.

"We didn't kidnap you. We took you before Oleg Sobakin's men could."

"Grabbing someone off the street, shoving her into a car, and drugging her is definitely kidnapping," I argue.

Though, I'm unsure why explaining the definition of kidnapping is more important than the part about why Oleg Sobakin—a known mafia leader—wanted me.

"Would you have taken my hand and skipped into the sunset with me if I had told you I was collecting your father's debt?" Kirya asks with a snort.

I fold my arms across my chest and curl my lip in disgust.

"Exactly." He flips the blade down and shoves the knife into his back pocket. "I knew you wouldn't come quietly, so I had to—"

"Kidnap me," I interrupt him.

"Jesus," he says, rubbing his forehead with exasperation. "I had no intention of collecting until—" He stops, glancing over his shoulder toward the door, as if he's expecting someone to be there. Maybe his friend from the BMW is coming back.

"Until what, Kirya?" I snap.

He turns around fast, cocking his head as he stares at me,

obviously not used to someone speaking to him like that. "I can offer you protection if you stay with me." There's a trace of desperation in his voice, as if he needs to convince me of something.

The final thread of hope I'd been holding onto evaporates. "You want to be my *krysha*?" I laugh at the suggestion. "What in the world would make you think I need protection? You know that I have no money, Kirya."

He laughs. "Yes, I know."

His smug laugh makes me sick, but I bite my tongue because I have a feeling I'm working on borrowed time. I know him well enough to know he won't stand for my attitude for long. "Then why are you offering me protection?"

"There is a price on your"—he pauses and looks me up and down—"head," he finishes.

His voice is flat, but the way he ogles me makes me shift uncomfortably. Excitement buzzes through me as his eyes scan my body, which makes me feel like a fool.

I should feel ashamed for being flattered by the gaze of someone who's holding me captive, but this is Kirya—and he's different. He's kind and funny and the only person outside of my family who truly cared for me. The only man I could ever trust when Vanya was gone.

Knowing he's mafia now should temper the old feelings his presence stirs inside me, but it doesn't. I remember the man he was before he got involved in this life, and it's stirring up a lust I haven't felt in years.

"Who would put a price tag on my head? I don't have anything that anyone would want."

"*You* may have nothing, but Vanya has millions now."

"What does that have to do with me? I don't have access to Vanya's money." I scowl. "He left me behind. As you can see."

The bitterness burns in my throat. My brother is in America, enjoying the freedom and extravagance of the West. Without me. I have none of his new life.

"It's not about you having access to his money. It's about him having the means to pay to stop anything from happening to you. That's why I'm offering my protection."

To stop anything from happening to me? My brain is finally putting together the puzzle pieces. Something will happen to me if I don't agree to Kirya's protection.

"Are you threatening me?"

"No. But someone else will."

My throat is dry when I try to speak, but I manage to whisper, "I don't have money for protection. I told you that, Kirya."

"You call me Kirya now." He chuckles. "Does that mean you trust me?"

I've always trusted him, but I won't admit that to him right now. Not when I don't know his motives. Not when he's holding me here against my will under the ruse that I can leave if I want.

"I trust you to tell me the truth. You and your friend grabbed me and stuffed me into a car. You bound my hands, drugged me, and left me in this cold, dark basement. I'm starving. I'm sore." I sigh and close my eyes for an extra beat. "And I'm scared."

When he reaches out and tries to touch my forehead, I cringe and back away.

"I'm sorry, Stasya," he says softly, lowering his hand. "I didn't mean to hurt you."

"If that were true, you wouldn't have done all of this to me. You are like family, Kirya. I would have talked to you." Keeping my voice strong is hard when all I want to do is sink to the floor and cry.

"There was no time to talk." Warmth floods his eyes,

reminding me of the old Kirya—the one who always looked out for me. "Stasya, I wasn't lying when I said you are free to go. But if you choose to leave, you will be kidnapped by very dangerous people. They will torture you until your brother pays them money."

Money runs the world. Especially now, when the stable—if not boring—life we've known is unstable and lawless. And some people who have been living without money for generations will do anything to get it. Everyone needs it and everyone wants it.

Mafia extortion isn't a surprise—but I never imagined I'd be involved.

Since Gorbachev's economic reforms, the stability we're used to is gone. With the restructuring, we've seen enough to realize that we've been a depressed, sheltered people for so long. The streets of Moscow—probably the entire country—are a free-for-all, for those who know the right people and have the money to bribe to get what they need.

The mafia has both—money and people under their thumb. They always win.

"They won't be kind, Stasya," Kirya continues. "You won't be having a rational conversation like this. They don't know you. They don't care about you. All they care about is Vanya's money. They will beat you and rape you without mercy. They will enjoy doing it. They will take pictures and videos and they will send them to your brother."

Fear sends a shiver from head to toe.

He's not lying, this I know. I've witnessed the heinousness of the mafia—even before he kidnapped me. I've seen cars stop, grab someone in broad daylight, and speed away. I've seen black BMWs roll down their windows and shoot others dead on the street right in front of me as I was walking home from the metro. I've stepped over dead bodies, swallowing back vomit as I watched their blood gush from their wounds and seep into the snow.

The reality of Kirya's words hit me harder than the bus that killed Mama five years ago. No matter what I do—I'm screwed.

Once you're a mafia target, you're as good as dead.

It's a matter of *when*, not *if*.

Ever since I found out Vanya defected, I've been wallowing in self-pity and anger because he didn't take me with him as he always promised he would.

But extortion never crossed my mind. Which is completely stupid. I should have realized the mafia would demand their cut of any Russian making money—especially American dollars.

An icy tingle causes the hair on my arms to raise and I swallow the bile rising in my throat as I realize the hopelessness of my situation.

My brother's choice to defect to the USA for freedom and money didn't just affect him—it sealed my fate as well. A future that holds either relentless torture leading to death—or being Kirya's property.

"As long as Vanya is playing hockey in America, they're always going to want his money, yes?" As I speak, Kirya nods, pressing his lips into a grim line. "They won't stop going after it. Whenever you let me go, they will come after me," I say, connecting the dots in my head out loud, so he knows I understand the situation I'm in. "I'm trapped with you forever."

"Trapped?" He winces. "Would you rather be safe with me or dead out there?" His jaw tightens, waiting for me to answer.

My eyes narrow. "It depends on what 'be safe with' you means."

"'It depends' is not the answer I expected." He laughs, but

it's not menacing. It's light, a reminder of the old times. "You'd rather be dead than be my lover?"

"The whore of a mafia thug," I say dryly. "Sounds like a wonderful life."

"Whore?" He reels back as if I slapped him. I didn't know mafia men had so much emotion over derogatory words. "What makes you think so little of me, Stasya? You didn't always feel this way."

"You're asking me to give you my body in exchange for something. That's the definition of a whore."

"While it's true I want you to be mine, Stasya, I'd never force you to fuck me. I'm not desperate." He smirks. "If you choose to be with me, you'd be my queen, not my whore."

"If I *choose*," I repeat softly.

We both know I don't have a choice.

"Let's pretend Sobakin doesn't kidnap you," Kirya steps back. "Is going home a better choice? Do you live without fear now? Your father won't stop taking his anger out on you. His wife is dead. His beloved son left without consulting him. And now he's stuck with you—the daughter he's always hated. The girl who makes him sick because you remind him of what he's lost." He paces back and forth in front of me as he ticks off the truths of going home.

"Please stop." It comes out as a whisper because I can't deny it. He's absolutely right.

"Just think." Kirya stops in front of me. "You'd never have to worry about anything again. You'd never worry about Vanya. You'd never have to work or wait in line for food or clothing." He reaches out and tilts my chin up until my gaze meets his. "Your father will never beat you again."

I glance at the scar that slices his left eyebrow in half before shaking his hand away and dropping my gaze to the floor.

Seeing the wound fills my heart with shame because it was my fault. I remember the night it happened so well, it feels like it was yesterday.

AFTER HANGING MY COAT AND SCARF ON THE COAT RACK IN THE hallway and changing into my slippers, I stopped at the kitchen where Babushka and Maria Androvna, a member of one of the other families that live on our floor, were working at their respective tables across from each other, as they had for as long as I could remember.

Irina, Kirya's mother, would be home soon, bringing fresh fish to fry on one of the four stoves, and our families would share everything the women made. As co-tenants who have lived together for so long, it's a natural part of life to share what we have and eat together. The sweet smell of borscht and loaves of freshly baked bread made my stomach growl. All I had for lunch was a small bowl of okroshka—a soup Babushka makes from leftovers.

"I'm so hungry, I could eat two of those loaves by myself," I teased the old women.

"What do you know about hunger?" she scoffed. "Did you live through the Great War?"

"Here we go," I mumbled under my breath and rolled my eyes.

Let it be clear, I wasn't poking fun at the war or the horrible Soviet tragedies that occurred during it. I was annoyed at how serious my grandmother makes everything—even a silly joke.

"That is not being a good communist, Stasya." She lifted the ladle from the borscht and pointed to the portrait of Vladimir Lenin, father of Communism, hanging on the wall over the stoves. It's the same portrait you'd see in every Russian household. I was pretty sure they were built into the walls during construction.

"Will Comrade Lenin send his ghost to haunt me, Babulya?" I

moved toward her slowly with my arms raised in front of me, as if I'm a spirit coming to get her.

"You'd do well to pray for his ghost! Better than sending KGB!" she said, then looks at Lenin's picture again as if it may be concealing a camera and spying on our every move.

It's not such an outlandish thought. Reality breeds paranoia.

"You're going mad, Olenka." Maria Androvna shook her head as she chopped onions.

Babushka shot her a dirty look before turning back to her borscht.

I laughed and backed out of the room, rubbing my hands together to warm them up as I walked to our room. When I entered, Papa was at the table, watching television and snacking on a plate of pickles. He was holding a glass of vodka in one hand and a photo of my mother in the other.

He glanced over his shoulder, scowling when he realized who entered the room. I was used to that kind of reaction. After Mama died, I became the sole target of his anger and resentment. It was funny how much he pretended to love her now that she's gone, yet when she was here, all he did was hit her and yell at her. Even though she had a better job and had more connections than he ever did. Maybe that was the reason he was so hard on her.

He tossed the photo on the table. "What do you do around here, Anastasiya? What do you bring to the family?" Papa asked. He's picking a fight, something I'd usually ignore in his drunken state, but I had a hard day at work and I was unable to hold my tongue.

"Well, I was the one who went out with Nikolai, so his father would save us that television you're watching before it went on the shelf at the store, so I guess I brought that to the family."

Papa jumped to his feet and rushed toward me. I raised my arms to block my face, so he punched me in the side of the head instead. I slapped his chest and tried to push him away, but he persevered, landing a few more blows before I fell to my knees.

"Papa! Sto—!"

He kicked me in the stomach, cutting off my plea for mercy. I was doubled over in pain, shaking and trying to catch my breath. My arms trembled, waiting for the next attack.

"Enough!" Kirya commanded as he burst into the room.

My head snapped up, surprised at hearing his voice. He moved out of the apartment over a year ago, and hadn't come around for months.

"This is not okay, Mikhail Grigorovich. You cannot hurt her anymore." He grabbed my father and whirled him toward the table. Papa reached out to brace himself, sending the pickle plate crashing to the floor. His shoulders heaved as he stood up.

He stared at Kirya, his black, rage-filled eyes narrowing with each heavy breath. "What happens in my family is none of your business." He grabbed the vodka bottle and smashed it against the table, then charged Kirya.

I tried to scream, but no sound came out. The simple act of breathing hurt so badly, I felt dizzy. I pushed myself back, resting against the wall as I watched the two men struggle, silently rooting for Kirya to win.

He easily pushed off Papa's attack, sending him into the wall, but my father wasted no time rushing him again. He wielded the jagged glass, slashing Kirya across the face. Blood spurt out, splattering on me.

I cried out in pain and fear, but Kirya wasn't phased. If anything, it brought him strength. He roared through clenched teeth and pummeled Papa with both fists, not letting up until my father dropped to the floor—inches from me. Even then, my neighbor doesn't stop, kicking relentlessly until Papa was an unmoving lump.

"If I ever find out you hurt her again, I will kill you." Kirya's voice was smooth, cold—frightening. "That is a promise."

I lifted my gaze slowly and scanned my childhood friend, from his scuffed black boots to his black jeans and leather jacket. Where in the world had he gotten that?

Our eyes met for a split second before he rushed out of the room. His heavy footsteps pounded through the hallway, getting lighter and lighter until I couldn't hear them anymore.

I stared at my father with absolutely no remorse for the happiness humming through my veins.

Babushka, *who had been watching in horror from the doorway, rushed into the room, bypassing my father and falling to her knees in front of me. She slid one arm across my shoulder and tilted my chin up gently with her other hand.*

"Are you all right, Stasya? Can you walk?" she asked.

I nodded, though I honestly wasn't sure if I could. Pain seared through my abdomen when she tried to help me to my feet. She may be short in stature, but she's one of the strongest women I know.

Once I was upright, she grabbed a blanket from the couch and wrapped it around my shoulders. Biting back the pain, I let her guide me across the hall to Maria Androvna's room. The two women wrapped my ribs tightly with cheesecloth while I did everything I could to keep from screaming from the excruciating pain.

I wish I would have said something—anything—to Kirya before he stormed out of the apartment that night. It was last time I saw him before tonight.

"I could kill him if you'd like." He leans closer, scanning my eyes for permission. I'm inhaling his sweet, minty breath every time he speaks. "I've wanted to do it for years."

Rage rises in my heart, rekindling the darkness I've kept buried deep inside. I've wished death on my father so many times I've lost count. Anything to keep him away—to stop him forever.

This Kirya, the cold-blooded gangster, could be my hero
—again.

He smirks. "He's not going to last long in the new Russia
anyway, Stasya. He puts his nose places it shouldn't be.
Gambles with the wrong people. Lies to the wrong people." He
dips his head lower, his lips inches from my ear when he whispers, "Hurts the wrong people."

I don't know if it's fear, lust, or an involuntary reaction to the
memory of the night Kirya saved me from my father's wrath
that makes my lips tremble. All I know is I desperately want to
kiss him. If I turn my head, our mouths will touch. Every part of
my brain is telling me to do it—to press my lips to his. I swallow
hard, fighting the urge.

Suddenly, he snakes one arm around me, spins me quickly
so my back is against his chest, and grips me firmly against him.
Fear strangles a surprised gasp in my throat.

"Stop!" I spit through clenched teeth while struggling to
break out of his grasp.

Instead of releasing me, he clutches me tighter, digging his
fingers into my side. His free hand flies from his back pocket to
my neck. The blade flips out, scratching my skin with every
quick, sharp breath I take.

"Keep grinding your ass into me, Stasya," he rasps against
my ear. "It feels good."

A tear slips down my cheek. This time, it's fear, not lust,
making me tremble. And my terror excites him. It's evident by
his hard length pressing against my back.

What had I done to make him lash out so quickly?

Just as I was starting to see the Kirya I used to know, the
man I trusted with my life, everything flipped.

I don't know this monster holding me at all.

7

KIRYA

I feel Anastasiya's throat jump, as if she's going to say something, but before she has the chance, the door swings open and Stanislav and Igor burst in. They're wearing black masks, concealing their identities until I decide it's safe to remove them.

"There you are," Igor says, as if me holding a knife against a woman's throat is as normal as watching *The Irony of Fate* on New Year's Eve. "That's the sister."

"I'm aware," I say dryly.

Stasya's heart beats rapidly. The quick rise and fall of her chest shakes my arm, causing the sharp, cold metal to dig into her skin. I know exactly how to hold my knife so it produces panic, not harm. Though I hate putting her through this, she needs to feel this fear so she understands the weight of her situation.

If she denies my protection, she's dead.

"Sobakin's men are going crazy." Igor sneers, revealing

crooked yellow teeth. "I told Slava how funny it was watching that piece of shit Vaz try to keep up with us."

We recruited Igor from a martial arts studio we get a lot of guys from. We want fighters—people angry with the system and willing to take matters into their own hands to get what they want.

But those men come with a past and I don't know Igor's yet. I don't trust him, which is exactly why I have him working directly with me and Slava. I'll keep him close until I can figure him out. There's something about him that makes internal alarms go off, but I can't pin down the reason.

Slava taps his temple. "A room full of smarts, where the key is lost."

I grunt, but keep my hold on Stasya firm until I send Igor away. The less interaction he has with her, the better. "Prostakov! Bring the car around to the back. Slava will wait there and let me know when you arrive."

Igor exits as soon as he's directed, but Slava hesitates.

"Why the fuck are you still standing there?" I ask.

He checks the door, making sure Igor is out of range before asking, "What are you going to do with her?"

"Anastasiya and I have come to an agreement, haven't we?" I ask her. When she nods, I loosen my grip, but she's still rigid under my hands. "I'm taking her to my flat."

"For fuck's sake, Kirya!" He rubs his face with both hands. "What are you doing?"

Stanislav—Slava—Rybakov is the one person outside of my family I trust with my life. Best friend shit aside, he's still required to obey my orders and decisions without question.

I let out a breath and release Stasya. She rounds her shoulders, casts her gaze downward, stepping backward, as if trying to sink into the wall. When she looks up, her eyes are wide and full of terror. It's the same reaction she has for her father after he hits her.

There is only one soft spot in my heart—and it belongs to her. I never wanted her to look at me like that, but I'll make it up to her. Once we're alone, I'll explain.

"It's the only way to keep her safe from Sobakin."

"Her safety is the last thing you should be worried about," Slava huffs, rolling his eyes.

"I don't remember asking for your opinion."

"Don't worry. You don't have to ask for me to give it to you."

"From this moment, Anastasiya Mikhailovna Kravtsova is a free woman, but she is mine." My voice is hard, so there is no misunderstanding. "She is to be protected at the highest level. Do you understand?"

Slava nods, straightening his shoulders, like a soldier receiving orders from his superior. No matter how long we've been friends, he knows where he stands in the hierarchy.

"Any and all interaction with her goes through me first. Do you understand?"

He nods again.

"I will speak to Igor myself, but I expect you to watch him, especially when it comes to Stasya."

He glances at the door. "I don't trust him, Kirya. We need to discuss it before you allow him to be alone with her."

"There is no discussion needed. He is *never* to be alone with her."

Slava shifts his eyes to Stasya, who's still breathing heavy, her heart pumping with fear. "Does Viktor know?"

"Know what? That she's with us?" I ask, playing dumb. "Yes."

"But does he know she is your weakness?" he asks in

English. Slava always tells it like it is. It's a quality I love and hate about him.

The language switch puts Stasya on alert. She leans forward, narrowing her eyes, as her fear gives way to curiosity. I understand her distrust, but I can't explain everything to her right now. We'll have time for that later.

"Go check to see if Igor is here," I command.

He nods and exits quickly.

Slava'ss right, but this isn't the time for the discussion.

"I want your decision, now, while we are alone," I tell Stasya.

"You made my decision," she responds. "You told them we'd come to an agreement."

"I have to do things to keep rank in front of my men, Stasya. But the choice is yours."

She looks around the room, but her posture says she's tired and defeated. "I assume your flat is nicer than this—or any room Sobakin will have me in."

I bite the inside of my cheek to hide my smile. "You're coming with me? That's your choice?"

"I didn't plan on dying today. Selling my soul seems like a better option."

"Maybe someday you won't see it that way," I say, taking her hand and leading her to the door. I'm not proud of the way I handled this situation, but I had to make her understand.

Stasya pauses before we move into the hallway. "I have one request."

"What's that?"

"I want to go home first."

I grab her arm. "If you think this is a game, you are mistaken. This is real. I can't change your circumstances, but I can protect you from the worst."

She glares at me. Jaw tight. Eyes cold. "I am accepting your protection, Kirya, but I *will* be allowed to go home and get some of my things."

"I'll send Slava to gather your things this week."

"No! I'm not compromising on this." She holds firm. "Slava cannot possibly know where I keep all of my most treasured possessions."

I wonder what kind of treasured possessions could she possibly need so badly. She and her family have nothing.

"Fine. But I'm going in with you."

"Fine," she agrees. I half-expect her to stick her tongue out at me like a petulant child.

Anastasiya Kravtsova never ceases to surprise me. Even with teased, blonde hair that makes her look taller than she is, she barely comes up to my neck. A gust of wind would probably blow her slight frame over. But she has more fire blazing inside her than a hearth in January. I thought she would be scared of me, but she's not. She's hard and fierce, making demands like she has the upper hand.

It's stupid—and so fucking sexy.

Maybe someday she'll realize my motives are pure. The only thing I care about is her safety. It's all I've ever cared about since the first time I heard her cry as the result of her father's hand.

Once we're alone, I can explain. I can ease her mind. I'm not much different than the Kirya she knew before.

More leather, less fear.

Before we exit, I retrieve a blindfold out of my back pocket and spin around to face her, lifting it to her eyes.

"What's that for?" She steps back, eyeing it with anger.

"Safety. I can't let you see where we are or where we're going."

"Enough of this, Kirya!" she says, slapping the blindfold out of my hand. She straightens her shoulders, raises her head, and looks me in the eye. I've woken the beast inside and I like it. "I made my choice and I don't plan on going back on it. You told Slava I was a free woman. The only time a woman should have a blindfold on is if you're surprising her with something wonderful."

"Remind me to blindfold you in my bedroom," I tease. I can't help it. Stasya's feisty side has my cock rock hard and pressing against my zipper.

"You wish," she says through clenched teeth as she elbows past me into the hallway.

I'd never seen Anastasiya stand up to her father. Not in all the years he beat and berated her. Yet, here she is with me— someone who could do far worse things than he ever could— standing toe-to-toe and giving me orders.

She's the epitome of a strong Soviet woman, but not the wrinkly, weathered *babushka* Westerners conjure. She is young and beautiful—a woman who grew up in times of extreme and difficult change. Despite years of being broken and beaten, she developed the strength of a lioness, yet kept her kind heart.

I always knew the lioness was there, and I'm going to help her embrace it. If there was ever a flicker of doubt in my mind my old neighbor was my soulmate—it's extinguished.

Stasya was born to be my queen.

8

STASYA

*S*lava waits in the car in front of my apartment on *2-Ya Kabel'naya Ulitsa*. Walking in with Kirya seems normal, as if there hasn't been an almost ten-year gap since the last time we'd done it.

As soon as we enter, I unwrap my scarf and begin to slide my shoes off, but Kirya stops me saying, "We won't be long."

I nod and walk confidently through the cluttered hallway, steeling myself for my father's wrath. I can't imagine he cared much that I didn't come home last night, but that doesn't mean he won't chastise me for it.

My head aches from whatever Kirya drugged me with and the mixture of smells coming from the kitchen. My stomach lurches, but I continue. It will take some time for all of this to hit me, but right now, I'm intent on grabbing my things and getting away from my father.

Papa is at the table watching television when I slip inside. He looks up with glassy eyes and sneers. "Look! The whore is home!"

I wince at the name—because he's right. That's exactly what I'm agreeing to by being with Kirya, but responding will only encourage him, and I don't want to hear it, so I keep my mouth closed and head straight for the balcony. Vanya must have an old hockey bag in storage out there.

As I riffle rapidly through the items stuffed into a water-proof bin, I look up quickly and watch Kirya step into the room. His large, intimidating frame fills the doorway.

The chair legs scrape against the floor as Papa jumps up. "What are you doing here?" he spits at Kirya. "Get out! Get out of here!"

"I had to bring Anastasiya to where the dog is buried before she can make peace and move forward."

Once I've found a bag, I silently move through the room, stuffing my things into it. I'm not bringing everything I own, just a few essentials—clothes to get me through a few days and treasured items I've saved through the years.

Papa narrows his eyes at Kirya. "Oh, you think you are a big pine now, don't you? Coming in here with your chest puffed, spouting shit about me being the problem? *You* are the problem!"

He's unfazed by Papa's lashing, seemingly bored when he responds, "Sit down and shut up before I beat your ass again, old man."

Papa snatches the vodka from the table and my pulse pounds. I don't want another fight like the one they had the last time Kirya was here. Not that my father doesn't deserve it, I'm just ready to put all of that behind us.

My heart thrashes inside my chest. I bite my lip, and hurry to collect things that have personal value. I can make more clothes; I can't get back photographs and mementos from better times. Once I'm finished, I stand next to Kirya.

"Put your things down, Anastasiya," Papa commands. "You are not going with him."

Kirya starts to speak, but I place my hand on his forearm. "It's my choice, Papa. I trust Kirya."

"You trust him?" My father's eyebrows narrow. "You trust a murderer?"

"Where's *Babushka*?" I ask, ignoring his questions. How does a daughter explain that she trusts a murderer more than she trusts her own father?

"You tell me," Papa responds.

I sigh, annoyed with his games. "Is she down the hall? I'd like to say goodbye."

"She isn't here. I haven't seen her since yesterday."

"What?" I glance at Kirya, who doesn't speak, just takes the bag out of my hand and secures the strap on his shoulder.

I've tried to keep my composure, because I've learned to handle anything my father throws at me, but if *Babushka* is missing, that changes everything.

"You see? He knows where she is! He kidnapped her!" Papa tightens his grip on the bottle and lunges at Kirya.

Instead of engage, Kirya pushes me out the door and yanks it shut behind us. A loud crash tells me Papa must've smashed the bottle anyway. I'm sure it was empty, because he'd never waste vodka on me.

"Olga is fine," he says, striding quickly down the hall.

My body relaxes with relief. It's all I need to know right now. I can ask questions about *Babushka's* whereabouts later.

As soon as we climb into the car, Slava speeds away. The building I've lived in my entire life gets smaller and smaller the further away we drive from it. I half-expected to see Papa running after us. Then I remember who I'm thinking about. My father hasn't cared about me since the day I was born. He got Vanya, the boy he wanted, four minutes before me.

"Why didn't you tell him you were collecting on his debt?" I ask, still staring out the window, mentally saying goodbye to the street I grew up on.

"I didn't need to," Kirya says. "You told him you chose to be with me."

I bite my bottom lip.

He's right. And I did it without any hesitation.

Because being with Kirya—a man entangled with the mafia —is still a safer and more welcome option than living one more minute with Papa.

I rest my head on the frame of the car and look out the window, watching Moscow go by and wondering if Vanya realizes his decision to have a better life turned mine completely upside down.

* * *

KIRYA SHAKES MY SHOULDER GENTLY, ROUSING ME OUT OF SLEEP. "We're home."

I lift my head from the frame and wipe the side of my mouth, hoping I hadn't been drooling. Then I scoot across the seat and climb out of the car, silently cursing myself for falling asleep. I planned on watching the route, but as soon as Slava started driving, I drifted off.

I knew Kirya would live in a nicer neighborhood than I did, but I never expected him to live right in the center of the city, in the theatre district, no less, minutes away from the Kremlin and Red Square. I almost can't believe my eyes.

"You live in the *Tverskoy* District?" I ask.

"Yes," he answers.

"Wow," I murmur, unable to hide my astonishment. I've never dreamed of visiting someone in an apartment here, let alone get to live in one.

Since Kirya didn't stop to admire his own neighborhood, he's a few feet ahead of me. I rush to catch up.

When we reach the fifth floor, he opens the door to reveal an apartment unlike anything I've ever seen. Not only is it spacious, it feels like I've stepped into a room in the Hermitage. Oversized, ornate, gold frames encasing remarkable artwork adorn the muted red walls and every piece of extravagant furniture looks antique, as if it were taken straight from the Tsar's collection. I've never seen a home decorated like this.

"You live here alone?" I ask, running my fingertips over a soft, gray, tufted couch.

"Yes," he answers, leading me down a hallway. "It was my uncle's apartment. He never married or had a family, so he left it to me when he moved to the United States."

I remember his uncle well. He was the one who brought Kirya and his mother black caviar on New Year's Day, and treats throughout the year. And he brought enough for the entire apartment. I always wondered what kind of life he led, but him living in a place like this was out of my imagination.

It's quiet and peaceful inside the apartment, which spooks me. I've never lived without some sort of chatter and commotion at all hours of the night. Or without the sound of Papa's snoring in the chair across the room from me.

"This is your room," Kirya says, holding the door open. I step past him and inside.

The space is just as luxurious as the rest of his apartment. I should take more time to appreciate the details, like the beautiful antique dresser and the magnificent art on the wall, but all I see is the bed. An actual bed! It's larger than the pull-out couch Vanya and I share and covered in a beautiful, purple blanket so fluffy it looks like it's stuffed with clouds.

I turn to Kirya, back to the bed, then back to him.

"Do you like it?" he asks. His amused grin and sparkling eyes tell me he's charmed by my excitement.

"Like it?" My cheeks hurt from the size of my smile. "I love it! It's the most beautiful thing I've ever laid eyes on."

"Then you've never looked in a mirror," he says.

Tonight, when I'm lying in this huge bed alone and not sure what to do with myself, I'll analyze his words, but I ignore it because there's only thing I want to do right now.

I bound toward the bed and jump onto it, landing on my belly with a flop. My face hits the softest, silkiest pillow I've ever touched, and I bury my nose in it. Maybe I should have asked for permission before jumping, but it's my very first time laying on a real bed, so I hope Kirya understands.

"Your dives used to be more graceful, Stasya." Kirya laughs. "Have you stopped swimming?"

My eyelids feel heavy, as if weights are holding them down. And this bed isn't helping the situation. If I stay like this, I'll be out within minutes.

I flip onto my back, basking in the luxurious cushioning underneath my body. The mattress seems to curve around my frame, something I never experienced with the flimsy trash that folds into the couch at my apartment.

I wonder if it's acceptable for a mafia queen to lay in bed all day, every day.

"How do you get anything done, Kirya?" I ask, ignoring his question about swimming. The sport I participated in for so long is a sore subject. One I'm not willing to discuss in front of this glorious beast I'm going to sleep on tonight.

He chuckles. "What do you mean?"

"If I had a bed like this, I would never get up," I say, stretching my arms and legs out as far as they can reach.

"Are you saying I have to join you in there if I want to see you?" Kirya asks, moving closer. He stops at the edge and sets a knee on the mattress, which sends me rolling toward him.

Butterflies burst in my stomach and my heartbeat accelerates. I'm exhausted, but not so much so that I'm not affected by his lean body looming over the bed. Still, no matter how much my heart betrays me, I'm resolute to keep my cool around Kirya.

"I slept on a nasty flat pull-out couch with Vanya for years. This will be the very first time I've slept in a bed. Can I have one night to myself before I have to take on my queenly duties?"

"You'll still be under my protection even if you're not under me." He abruptly removes his knee and retreats to the door. "I told you I won't force you to do anything, Stasya.

"I'm sure you'll find anything you need that you didn't bring from your apartment in the drawers and closet. The bathroom is down the hall—first door on the right."

"I—" I begin, bolting upright at his sudden attitude change. But Kirya doesn't wait for my response. He stalks out, slamming the door behind him.

What right does he have to be angry with me? Did he really think a soft bed and smooth words would make me spread my legs for him after what he put me through?

I'm the one who should to be angry. I'm the one who's a prisoner of shitty circumstances. Instead of crying my eyes out into this magnificent, downy pillow, I'm trying make the best of the situation.

Under different circumstances, I might be excited at reuniting with an old friend. My body certainly responded when I first saw him.

Kirya can be as moody as he wants. I've got other things to think about.

First things first. My bladder is about to burst and I need a shower. Though it's the last thing I want to do, I slide out of the bed and rush out the door. Once I'm in the hallway, I stop and look both ways, trying to remember if Kirya said the bathroom was on the right or left. I should have been listening instead of snuggling into the blankets.

I head left and peek into the first door, which is wide open. Kirya stands at the end of the big beautiful bed, naked from the waist up, removing the belt from his jeans. I've seen him shirtless on multiple occasions, but tonight is the second time it makes my breath catch.

The first time, I'd been leaning against the wall in the hallway behind Maria Androvna, waiting for my turn to use the bathroom, when the door opened and Kirya stepped out with nothing but a thin green towel wrapped around his waist. His muscles weren't as large or defined as they are today, but seeing his bare chest with water dripping down burned a hole in my memory. That was the moment he went from "just one of the neighbor boys" to "how have I never noticed the neighbor boy was this gorgeous?"

Just thinking about it makes me smile. I peek once more, taking in the huge tattoo of an angel-like figure holding a sickle in one hand and a lock in the other, and the way his beltless jeans hang low on his hips, revealing a tapered torso and two sexy back dimples.

He turns his head slightly, and I reel back, hoping he didn't catch me staring. The fear of getting caught is a tiny bit exciting though. What would he say if he found me appreciating his physique?

It must be the effects of the drugs rattling my head. Instead of risk getting caught, I turn around and shuffle to the bathroom. A quick shower will clear my mind for sleep.

* * *

SILENCE IS SCARY.

It's something I never realized before.

In my apartment, the hum of activity at all hours of the night usually soothes me to sleep. The only time I could escape it was summers at the *dacha*. But then, I had someone to sleep with.

For as much as we complain about communal living, there's something to be said about always having someone around. I guess it takes being alone and isolated in eerie silence to realize how comforting it really was.

My mind races, thinking about everything that happened over the last couple of days. From Vanya's defection to Dima's coldness to the absurdity of being kidnapped by my neighbor to stop me from being kidnapped by a ruthless mafia, who planned on torturing me and killing me if Vanya didn't pay them.

My life went from mundane to a dramatic crime movie.

After an hour of tossing and turning, praying for noise to drown out the loudness in my head, I slip out of bed and tiptoe down the hall. Kirya's door is still open, though the lights are off.

"Kirya," I whisper. I lean against the wall, wringing my hands and biting my lip, waiting for his answer. "Kirya!" I whisper again, louder this time.

Still no answer.

Who can sleep in this silence?

As quickly and quietly as possible, I cross the floor and slip under the covers. Thankfully, his bed is large enough that I'm fairly undetectable. If I hug the edge and stay on my side, he won't even know I'm here.

Exhaustion covers me like a cloak, wearing me down and enveloping me in that lovely lull right before sleep takes over.

My eyelids flutter.

My heartbeat slows.

The bed creaks.

I open my eyes and swallow hard.

Kirya wraps one arm around me and pulls me into his body. Despite never being in this position with him before, it feels familiar and safe. My back rests against his chest and the curve of my backside presses into his pelvis.

"Everything okay, kitten?" he whispers, pulling me closer.

The endearment makes me smile. It had to have been almost ten years ago when he told me I reminded him of a kitten.

When I asked him why, he said I always curled up in the chair under the window that had the most sunlight come through. And when I was outside, I'd close my eyes and lift my face to the sun. After that, he'd meow at me whenever he saw me acting cat-like. Because Kirya has always been a leader, all the other kids started meowing at me as well.

At the time, I didn't think anything of him noticing my patterns, but hearing him call me kitten brings the memories flooding back.

"I didn't mean to wake you. I was—" I pause, not wanting to admit my fear.

"Scared?" His chest rises, halts for a beat, then falls slowly.

I nod. "I've never slept in a room by myself before."

"You get used to it." His voice is barely a whisper.

I don't want to get used to it. Not when being wrapped into his arms and pressed against his body feels so good.

"Thank you for letting me sleep here," I say. "I promise to use the beautiful room you have for me tomorrow."

"My bed is your bed, Stasya," he says sleepily. "Anything I have is yours."

In this moment, everything is right. Tomorrow, I will face the consequences of my decision. But tonight, I relax to the sound of his heartbeat soothing me to slumber.

9

STASYA

When I wake up, the space Kirya occupied last night is empty. The blankets are drawn back, sheets wrinkled where his body once lay. I never wake up in an empty bed after falling asleep in his arms in any of the silly, teenage daydreams I used to have about him. Still, the proof of his presence feels like victory.

Until I sit up and the euphoria quickly gives way to a painful headache. My body feels like it weighs a thousand kilos. Though I got a good amount of rest, I'm still groggy and tired.

Being drugged by the man I've fantasized about my entire life isn't the way I wanted to start off a courtship.

Kirya and I are going to have to have a talk. If he thinks his mafia tricks are an acceptable way to treat someone he considers a friend, he's about to have a fight on his hands. And this one will be right here on his turf.

He made a comment about having to do it because he didn't think I would go with him. If Kirya ran up to me on the streets of Moscow and told me a gang was in the car behind me, planning on kidnapping me, I think I would have trusted him enough to go with him without being drugged.

I mean, as pathetic as it sounds, I probably would have gone with him when he told me he won me in a bet. If Papa thinks I'm so worthless, that he was willing to give me up in a card game, why wouldn't I go? At least I'd be with a friend who respected me. I'm not saying I wouldn't have been angry or hurt, but it would have given me an out.

And isn't that what I've been looking for? Isn't that the reason I was so desperate for Vanya to take me to the United States if he ever got the chance to go?

To get out of my situation.

Vanya. My dear Vanya. I twist the green blanket on my lap. Despite my anger, I miss him terribly. Deep down in my heart, I know he didn't mean for any of this to happen. But whether he meant for it to happen or not, it did. And now I'm left trying to figure out if I can trust an old friend whose path took a drastic turn since we last met.

Kirya's life is the stuff nightmares are made of. Murder, violence, torture, but there's no doubt he has power—and connections. Maybe he has a way to get me in contact with my brother. I just need to hear his voice. Hear that he's okay.

With a new mission, I slide out of bed and drag myself to the bathroom. Last night, I'd been too exhausted to notice all the small details in Kirya's home. A single person living in a four-room apartment alone baffles my mind. It goes against everything I've ever known.

If there is space, why are there so many people waiting for apartments from the government? Why doesn't Kirya have other families living with him? At the very least, I thought his mother would live with him. She moved out of the room across from ours two years ago. If she isn't with her son, where is she?

When I turn on the light, various beautiful things catch my eye at once, shining like diamonds. The bathroom is stocked with anything a person could ever want. Fluffy white towels are stacked on a shelf adorned with a vase of gorgeous lilacs.

I pick up a bar of soap from the plastic dish on the sink and bring it to my nose. It smells like fresh lavender—my favorite scent. I clutch it in my hand, as if it will disappear when I turn my back to run the shower.

Last night's shower felt good because of how dirty and cold I was, but I was so tired and disoriented, I didn't fully appreciate it. Today, the simple act is absolute heaven. As I rub the smooth, lavender soap over my skin, something hits me.

I can be in here as long as I want. There's no one timing me. No one pounding on the door, cursing at me to hurry up.

I feel like a foreigner in my hometown.

I've had the same tattered, tan towel since I was a little girl. It's see-through and smells like fish from being hung to dry on one of the clotheslines cutting through the kitchen. I've never seen a towel like the beautiful, fluffy ones stacked on the shelf.

Unable to contain my giddiness, I grab one and throw it over my shoulders, taking an extra beat to enjoy the softness. After drying off the rest of my body, I wrap it around me and tuck in the corner to secure it above my breasts.

Water drips from my hair onto my shoulders and down my back. Without thinking, I reach for another towel, then catch myself. It's wasteful to use another one just for my hair. But it's there, and I need to get back to my room without dripping all over the beautiful wood floors.

I'm not sure what being Kirya's girlfriend entails, but I have a feeling I'll be the one washing any towels I use. Since I don't mind doing laundry, I decide to use the extra towel and appreciate the luxury this one time.

A rap on the door startles me out of my thoughts. I clutch the towel around my chest with both hands.

"Anastasiya?" a voice calls.

I place my hand on the bathroom door to steady my shaky knees, then swallow back panic and ask, "Who's there?"

"It's Slava," he says gruffly. "You have nothing to worry about. You're safe with me."

"Safe," I whisper. It's an uneasy feeling after living with my guard up my entire life. I've always been on edge, waiting for Papa's next outburst. I've never known what it feels like to be completely safe.

"I didn't mean to frighten you. I just wanted to let you know I was here so you weren't surprised when you came out."

His thoughtfulness slightly softens my cool attitude.

I like Slava already. Walking out in my towel in front of someone other than Kirya would have been totally awkward. Respect for my modesty was the last thing I expected from a mafia thug.

"Thank you," I tell him, then pause before adding, "I'm ready to come out now, so can you—"

"Of course!" he says quickly. "I'll be in the living room."

I wait until I can't hear his footsteps anymore before slipping out of the bathroom and hurrying to my room. I dress quickly and drop the towels on the floor next to the door. Slava can show me to the laundry area later.

"Where's Kirya?" I ask, fastening my necklace as I enter the living room.

Sunlight filters through the massive windows, both brightening and warming the room. Though lavish and extravagant, it's comfortable and lived-in. For a moment, I wonder how Kirya got all the beautiful art adorning the apartment. Then I realize I might not actually want to know the answer.

Slava sits on the couch with his feet on a glass table. He looks up from the TV. "He had a few meetings in Nizhny Novgorod today, but he'll be home tonight—probably late."

"You look familiar. Have we met before?" I ask, peering at him.

When we were young, kids were always running up and down the hallways, whether on our floor or another in the high-rise complex. Maybe Slava was one of them.

One thing I will never complain about is my childhood. As an adult, I can look back and see what I missed out on. But I was a very happy kid. Life was simple, innocent. You don't realize what you're missing if you never had it in the first place.

"No," he says firmly.

It takes me a few tries, but I finally find a cupboard with plates and glasses. "You're sure?" I ask, filling a cup with water.

"Unless you used to visit men in prison, I'm certain we have never met, Anastasiya."

"What were you in prison for so young?"

"Stealing. Fighting. I beat a guy to death." Slava shrugs, as if telling me he murdered someone is as normal as talking about the weather.

It's another reminder of how sheltered I've been. Though everyone knows about the existence of the mafia and the boys in street gangs trying to be like mafia, I never thought much of them. I knew to stay away and mind my own business.

"You don't regret it?"

"Regret what?" He looks at me. "Prison? No." He shakes his head.

"Killing people?"

He stands, tugging his jeans up before coming toward me. He's only a bit taller than I am, but his biceps bulge under his black T-shirt. I can't help but think I've awakened a sleeping bear. Thankfully, there's a kitchen counter between us.

"I'd rather be the one killing than being killed, wouldn't you?"

"I don't think I could."

"What? Kill someone?" he asks, scanning my eyes. "You could do it if you had to." He places his hands on the counter and leans forward. "I saw you struggle and fight to survive when Kirya grabbed you. Can you honestly tell me you wouldn't have shot him if you had the means?"

"Honestly?"

He nods without taking his eyes off me.

"I don't know."

I gaze out the window next to the sink. In the winter, there are times when Moscow looks so ugly and dirty that I don't even want to get out of bed. And then there are days like today, when the sun illuminates the morning dew, giving the appearance of diamonds dangling on the tips of trees.

He smiles. "Panic, pain, fear, oppression—they all make people do things they never thought they would. We're nothing but animals with brains. We do what we must to survive," Slava says. "That's why you're here, yes?"

"What's the good in surviving if you can't live?" I ask.

Living is being able to walk the streets alone without fear. Is it living if I have to have a bodyguard and look over my shoulder for the rest of my life? Will I ever truly be able to live again?

The tea glass on the counter must be his because he picks it up and sips it. Slava is a stocky man with huge muscles and multiple tattoos, but sipping tea in a luxurious Moscow apartment, he looks almost bourgeoisie. "Kirya was right about you."

"What was he right about?"

"You're very smart, Stasya."

"What about you?" I change the subject. "What's your passion, Slava? If you could do anything, what would it be?"

"Tattooing."

It shouldn't be surprising, considering how many he has, but tattooing isn't really a career.

He continues. "I started doing it while I was in prison and got really good. It made me feel powerful to have a skill other people didn't, and to be better than the ones that did. I've always liked art, drawing."

"I draw too!" I say, happy to make a connection with him. "What are your plans today?"

"Watching you," he says dryly.

"Perfect!" I clasp my hands together, excited about the idea that popped into my head. I look around and open a few drawers in the kitchen. "Do you know where Kirya keeps the pencils?"

"No, but I have a strong feeling they wouldn't be in the kitchen utensil drawer."

I rush to the hallway toward Kirya's room, but hesitate before going inside. I don't feel comfortable going through his personal drawers without him here. Slava creeps into the hallway, eyebrows raised in interest.

"The last room on the right is an office." He nods. "He may have some shit in there."

The office of a mafia man could hold things I don't want or need to see. And no matter how interested I am to know what goes on, I can't bring myself to riffle through his belongings yet.

"I have a better idea! Let's run to the store and grab some notebooks and pencils. Then we can sit at *Park Zaryad'ye* and sketch."

"You're a barrel of fun, aren't you?"

"Well, you can't follow me to work, so I'm assuming I'm not going back to my normal life."

It's been three days since I showed up at the bank. Instead of wonder where I've been, I'm sure my coworkers have been cursing my name for sticking them with an extra load.

"Kirya has taken care of everything with your employer," he says. "And *we* need to go shopping."

"I just asked you to take me shopping!"

He rolls his eyes. "Real shopping."

"I have everything I need." I dismiss him.

"Actually, you don't. You're going to need dresses for when you go out with Kirya." He scans my outfit—a perfectly acceptable gray pencil skirt and oversized sweater. Which is very fashionable right now. "You can't wear that."

"Slava."

"Yes?" He looks up.

"Take me to a store where I can get pencils and notebooks." It's a long shot to try to give him a command, but as Kirya's girlfriend, he has to listen to me, right?

Slava crosses his arms over his barrel chest and straightens. "That was not part of the orders I was given."

I bite my lip, thinking for a minute before blurting out, "I'll let you give me a tattoo."

"What?" he asks, dropping his arms and leaning closer, as if he didn't hear correctly.

"If you go to the park and sketch with me, I'll let you give me a tattoo. Anything you want," I tell him, hoping it sweetens the deal. "But I get to pick the placement."

He eyes me with distrust, but shrugs. "Fine. Let's do this."

There was only one thing going through my head when I threw out the tattoo idea. I want to gain Slava's trust. If we establish that, he may give me more freedom—or a sense of freedom. I heard Kirya tell him I was a free woman, and if that's true, I can spend my newly-unemployed days how I want—not on orders from Kirya.

I understand the ultimate motive is to keep me safe, but I can't help but feel like a prisoner. Do I want the alternative of being picked up by Oleg Sobakin's gang? No. But being told what to do, where I can go, and the kinds of outfits I need to wear doesn't feel like freedom.

Hopefully, Slava and I develop a friendship. Because if we don't, my life with Kirya won't be any better than life with my father.

Having Slava's "protection" is nothing like I thought it would be. I thought he'd be by my side, walking around, intimidating people. I thought I'd have to make small talk and pretend it wasn't annoying and creepy having someone on my heels everywhere I go. But most of the time, I barely know he's there. He hangs out in my peripheral vision, and lets me do what I want.

He even let me call Svetlana to ask her to meet me for lunch at a restaurant. Though, using the words "let me" seems a bit harsh. When I asked, his exact words were: *"What are you asking me for? Do I look like your fucking father?"*

"Please excuse my appearance, my dear Stasya," she says, patting her dark curls. "I was so excited to hear from you, I came straight from work."

I stand up to greet her, kissing her on the cheeks. "You look lovely." Though her red pants are to die for, the first thing I noticed when she arrived was her jacket. It's one I made for her using one of Vanya's old hockey jerseys.

"I get so many compliments on this." She sits across from me. "Everyone wonders where I got such an interesting Scarlet Army coat. A Canadian man in Red Square even offered to buy it off me."

"You should have taken his money," I tell her.

"Never. I love your designs. People can pay *you* for them, not me. Which reminds me!" Svetlana spins around and digs in her purse. She slams a copy of *Burda,* our favorite women's fashion magazine, on the table and quickly flips the pages. "This! I need you to make this for me!"

She points to a beautiful, black, leather skirt with four thin, horizontal stripes. I pick up the magazine and bring it closer to see the photo better. The stripes look to be a red piping. "I could do that," I say, nodding with the confirmation.

"But where will you get leather?"

"My boyfriend has connections." I laugh, though it's only funny to me.

I glance at Slava quickly. Just as I was complimenting him, saying how cool he's been, there he is standing like a creepy stone gargoyle in the corner.

Can't he watch me from a table, drinking tea? Does he have to stick out like a—well, like a criminal?

"Boyfriend?" Svetlana asks, leaning closer. She looks Slava's way. "Is that him?"

"No!" I shake my head quickly as my skin bristles.

"Then why is that guy staring at you?"

"My boyfriend thinks I'm going to get kidnapped by the mafia so, he gave me a bodyguard."

Svetlana just stares at me with wide eyes, trying to figure out if I'm telling her the truth. She sets an elbow on the table and places her chin in her palm. "Can you repeat all of that? You sound absolutely insane."

"I'm sure you heard that Vanya defected?"

She nods and takes my hand quickly. "I'm sorry."

"I'm happy for him. It's hard, but I know he has a better life now." I look down, then back up at my friend. "Maybe I'll start thinking of myself as royalty. Then having someone following me around won't feel so uncomfortable."

"I think it's romantic," Sveta says dreamily. "Imagine having someone love you that much."

Some women find mafia men intoxicating because they want the luxuries that go along with the lifestyle.

I don't understand someone being so blinded by material things that they would sacrifice putting themselves in such danger for it. I'm not claiming Sveta is one of those women, but when she says having my boyfriend's protection is romantic, it makes me wonder.

Maybe I should invite Slava over to meet her.

"Two violent mafias are fighting over me because my brother didn't think about how his choice would affect his family." I roll my eyes. "Romantic is not how I'd describe it."

"I didn't mean it that way, Stasya. I'm sorry for—"

"No, Sveta," I interrupt, shaking my head. "I'm sorry. I didn't mean to be so rude."

The last thing I should be doing is taking out my anger on my oldest friend. Sveta is one of the only people who keeps me grounded. She's always been good to me.

"I don't know what it's like to be in your situation, my friend, but if you need me, I'm always here for you."

"I'm always here for you as well. And," I add, tapping the skirt from the magazine on the table, "I will dress you in the finest clothing. That's what friends are for."

10

KIRYA

*B*eing a player's agent is much easier than I originally expected it to be, especially without the theatrics of defection. The first few players I spoke with after Ivan Kravtsov snuck out of the Soviet Union had mixed feelings about his choice.

But after his heroic story of escaping a cruel, communist regime and is new lavish lifestyle got splashed across every newspaper and magazine in the West, he's considered a legend.

I don't even have to contact players anymore. They seek me out.

The Soviet system is imploding, even the Scarlet hockey machine, and no one wants to be buried under the rubble when it comes crashing down. A few of the older guys jumped at the chance to go to North America with that shitty Soviet-sport contract, but the younger guys didn't grow up with the same blind patriotism.

They grew up with dollar signs in their eyes, wondering: if

they are among the best players in the world, why aren't they paid the way players in the NHL are paid?

In the past, Soviet officials kept athletes on a tight rope when traveling, but even with the checkpoints in place to shelter them, there was no way they wouldn't notice the freedoms people outside of the Soviet Union had. Now that they've seen Vanya succeed, there's a rush to get out.

It's after midnight when I get home from Nizhny Novgorod. I'm so exhausted from the long day of driving, I know I'm going to be out like a light when my head hits my pillow.

But the trip was worth it because there are four guys from the team there who are looking at moving to the NHL. Three of them signed with me today, while one is holding out because he thinks things are going to open up for Soviet athletes to do everything themselves soon.

At first, it annoyed me that he refused to see the benefit of having someone else negotiate a contract on his behalf, especially with how savvy the NHL teams are. They've been fucking players out of money and benefits for generations.

But I respect his decision to try to do it himself because being screwed by the NHL is still better than playing for the Central Scarlet Army—where the compensation is a shitty monthly stipend and the pride of being a national hero.

And, hell, I'll take three out of four every time.

When I open the door, the glow of the TV screen startles me and I grab the gun at my hip. I'm so used to coming home to an empty apartment, I almost forgot Stasya was here.

Almost.

Waking up with her ass pressed against my cock this morning has been running through my mind all day. It took all of my power not to slide between her legs and wake her up with a huge surprise.

But I'd never take her that way unless she asked me to. I want her to want me.

It's not that I forgot she was here; I just didn't expect her to be sprawled across the couch sleeping when I walked in the door. I thought she'd be waiting for me in my bed.

After removing my shoes and coat, I walk quietly to the couch. Stasya looks like an angel. Her luscious lips are parted, forming an "O" shape. It stirs life into me.

I bend down and scoop her into my arms, cradling her against my chest. Her eyelids flutter open, but close again quickly. I'm actually glad she's so tired. I don't feel like fighting tonight.

Instead of taking her to her bedroom, I head straight for mine. If she doesn't like her sleeping arrangements, she'll move —as she proved to me last night.

Gently, I place her on the bed and pull the blankets over her. Her wavy, blonde hair covers her face, so I reach out and tuck it behind her ear. She looks lovely and innocent when she's sleeping.

There aren't many things I miss about communal living, but one is seeing Stasya every day. I've missed going to sleep every night knowing I'd see her bright beautiful smile the next morning. To me, she represents everything that's good with the world —even during gray Moscow winters where nothing was good.

She deserves an apology for the way all of this went down.

For months leading up to it, I'd been so consumed with making sure every detail was in place to make Vanya's defection go as smoothly as possible, I didn't even think about his family. Or, better said, I didn't think about the repercussions for his family.

I should have, because I know damn well if I hadn't been the one helping Vanya get out of the country, I would have been the one pounding on his door threatening him to pay for protection. And if he refused, I probably would have held his sister for ransom.

But not the way Sobakin would. I'd never hurt her. She'd be more likely to get annoyed with me doting on her before she ever feared for her life.

It's funny to think, even if this had happened differently, we'd be in the same situation we are right now.

The way I see it, no matter what twists and turns our lives took, Stasya was always meant to be by my side.

I climb into bed and scoot over until I'm right behind her, then wrap an arm around her and bring her in so we're as close as we can possibly be without being connected by my dick.

As I drift off to sleep, the only thing I can think about is how long I've waited for this moment. I've waited years to kiss her and I'll wait a hundred more if I have to. I want her to be with me because she wants to, not because she thinks I forced her.

* * *

THE NEXT MORNING, I'M DISAPPOINTED WHEN STASYA ISN'T IN MY bed when I wake up. I was hoping for a few quiet minutes with her where we could let our guards down. Apologizing doesn't come easy for me and that moment of naked vulnerability just before the sun comes up might help.

But a perfect scenario isn't in the cards today, so I get up, take a shower, and get dressed. When I enter the kitchen, I'm tucking my gun into the holster on my hip.

"Good morning, Cowboy," Stasya greets me dryly, eyeing my gun. She's sitting on the cushion in the living room window, hands wrapped around a glass of tea. "Do you always carry that?"

"No," I tell her honestly, glancing at the Glock. "Sometimes I carry my *Stechkin*."

There's no reason to lie since she's going to be around both of them a lot.

I blow out a stream of air as I reach for a tea glass. Time to suck up my pride. The sooner I apologize, the faster we can move forward.

"Look, Stasya. I know the way I handled things weren't ideal," I begin, avoiding her eyes by pouring hot water into my glass. "but I hope you understand why I had to do it that way."

"Actually," she interrupts, "I *don't* understand why you had to scare the shit out of me, drug me, and throw me in a dark, cold room. If I were going to save you from being kidnapped, I would have said"—she leans over and sets her tea on the floor—"'Kirya! I got to you just in time! There is group of bad men who want to hurt you in the car behind you." She waves me toward her animatedly. "Please jump in, and I'll take you somewhere safe.'"

She has a point. A point that never crossed my mind for a minute because it wasn't the original plan.

I scoop a few teaspoons of loose leaves into the strainer and drop it into my glass. "I did what I did because I wasn't sure if I was going to let you know I had anything to do with it," I admit quietly. "I was going to be the one to save you from the bad guys."

She calmly folds her hands together and sets them in her lap. "Excuse me?"

My chest tightens, but I push back the uneasy embarrassment and speak louder. "Being your hero sounded like the better way to get you to accept my protection. But I can't lie to you. I could never live with myself if I lost your trust."

She's quiet. Probably thinking about what I've gotten her

into. I don't blame her for being angry. If she ever forgives me, it will be a miracle. But I wasn't kidding when I said I can't lie to her. She deserves so much more than that.

"My life is dangerous, Stasya. The last thing I wanted to do was bring you into it."

"Then why did you?" she yells, jumping up. "Why did you bring me here?"

"Because I had no choice!" I slam a hand on the counter. "Once Sobakin set his sights on you, I had to do something. I knew you were more likely to accept protection if you trusted the person protecting you. You may not like me right now, but you trust me, yes?"

She stares at me without answering. I take a deep breath and scrub my face, rubbing my eyes with my fingers.

"You've always held a place in my heart, Stasya. I would never let anything happen to you. Do you believe that?"

She lifts her glass off the floor and takes a sip. Her silence is killing me. And patience isn't one of my virtues. "You promise never to lie to me?" she asks softly.

"I promise."

"I don't know how I'm going to handle this life, Kirya. I'm afraid of cars. I'm afraid of guns. Afraid of..." Her voice trails off.

Afraid of me.

She doesn't have to say it for me to understand. I know this isn't the life she ever expected to have. But I'll do everything in my power to make her comfortable.

"You just need to get used to everything. Come on." I wave her over to me, removing the pistol. "You're going to need to be relaxed around guns."

She stares at me without moving. I laugh and return the gaze. If she thinks she can win this contest, she has no idea who she's up against. I've stared down men ten times her size.

It hasn't even been thirty seconds when she breaks the eye contact with a huff. Scowling, she shuffles toward me, stopping to remove her glass from the *podstakannik,* the ornate silver glass holder, and set it in the sink.

If this were anyone else, I'd be laughing my ass off at the childish reaction, but I don't need her to be any more pissed at me than she already is, so I restrain myself.

I hold the gun out to her. She hesitates before taking it from my hand. She swallows hard, holding it as far away from her body as she can.

"Loosen up. Get a feel for it."

Damn. She looks super sexy gripping my automatic pistol, but her face is scrunched in fear.

"I've got the feel. And now I'm okay." She tries to hand it back, but I shake my head.

"Hold it with two hands, like this." I place her hands on the gun so she's holding it correctly. Then I raise her arms until the barrel is at my temple. "Guns are nothing to be afraid of." Her hands shake and the metal taps my skin. "It's the person holding the gun."

The terror in her eyes tells me it's time to stop. I'm supposed to be making her feel comfortable here.

"Get dressed." I take the gun and nod toward the hallway. "We'll go to lunch."

"Is that code for murder?" she asks, narrowing her eyes at me.

"It's not code for anything. I'm hungry."

She turns sideways, careful not to brush me as she passes.

Maybe having her hold a gun to my head was too much for our first morning together.

* * *

"Where did you get that dress, Stasya?" I ask, unable to take my eyes off her as she enters the living room. I'm already at the door, ready to meet Slava, who's waiting for us in the car.

She pulls her coat on, quickly covering the shabby, gray fabric. Her eyes are focused on the floor as if embarrassed. "It was one of *Dedushka's* old shirts," she says quickly. "I kept some of his clothes and made things for me and *Babushka*. It was a way to keep him close to our hearts."

I open her jacket to get a better look. "You made this?"

She nods.

"It's beautiful work." I lift my eyes to hers before tugging the coat closed. I should back away, but I don't. She smells like the French lavender soap I handpicked just for her. She watches intently as I fasten each button on her coat then grab a scarf from the rack next to the door and wrap it around her neck.

Her cheeks flush. "Thank you."

"Do you enjoy making clothes or did you do it to save money?" I hold the door open, allowing her to exit first.

"I love it. I have notebooks full of ideas. Drawings and measurements. But it's hard to find fabric. That's why I use old clothes. It feels good to take something no one else wants and make something beautiful out of it."

"That will change, Stasya. You're far too talented to use old clothes."

"I don't have time or money for—" she begins.

I grab her wrist and spin her around. She braces herself on my chest, her breath speeding up.

"You're with me now. You have the time to do whatever you want." My heart races, thinking about all the things I would give her if it made her happy. Her pulse pounds against my fingers. "I'll get you fabric from anywhere in the world. You want lace from France or silk from Japan? It's yours."

"It's too much, Kirya," she whispers without looking at me. "I couldn't take it."

Releasing her wrist, I step back to give her space. "I told you before, everything I have is yours. That includes money, Anastasiya. If you want something, all you have to do is say the word."

She nods stiffly.

Part of me hoped Stasya might forget about the drama of how she came to be with me, and slide right into my arms. Accepting her timeframe is going to be one of the hardest things for me. I'm used to people doing what I want when I say to do it.

But I can wait.

Stasya and I are destined to be together forever, which means time is something we have an infinite amount of.

11

KIRYA

*B*efore Stasya, I didn't take much time to relax. Laying on the couch and watching a movie never seemed important when there's so much work to be done outside of these apartment walls. I've spent more than ten years cultivating relationships and making a name for myself in the Moscow underworld.

And yet, I've come to enjoy the quiet evenings with Stasya curled up at my side. Maybe I don't have to spend all seven nights of the week working. Especially when the most important relationship to cultivate is the one right here.

"What's this?" Stasya eyes the silver box next to the TV with confusion. She leans closer, examining the buttons.

"It's a VHS player," I say, setting a bowl of popcorn on the table. "It plays movies."

Her eyes light up. "Really?"

"You still love going to the cinema, yes?" I ask.

It was always one of her favorite treats when we were young. She didn't get to go often, but I still remember the time

Mama asked her if she wanted to see a movie with us. I saw her in the hallway later that day, shining her scuffed boots. And when she came out to meet us, she had on her best dress. At the time, I thought she was crazy, but it's sweet to think about now.

"What kind of movies?" She's just about to sit down when I remember I forgot to bring the drinks.

I get up to press the play button on the VCR. "There's a surprise for you in the refrigerator. Grab us two while I get the movie started."

She skips to the kitchen. I hear the audible gasp after she opens the door.

"Pepsi Cola!" she squeals. "Six of them!"

I laugh and settle back on the couch. She hasn't stopped talking about Pepsi since she and Slava stopped to buy one from a street vendor last week. Seeing how little things, like having her favorite cola in the apartment, makes her happy brings warmth to my chest. I'm proud to be able to provide the things she wants and needs.

"Thank you," she gushes, as she rushes back to the couch with two cold, glass bottles. "You are the most thoughtful man!" She drops a kiss on my lips and hands me a drink before curling up next to me.

"What are we watching?" she asks, wiggling closer. I put an arm around her shoulders.

"It's an American movie." I scratch my head, trying to remember the name. "*Back to the Future*, I think."

Stasya looks puzzled. "That doesn't make any sense."

I pinch her side and she laughs. "Let's watch and find out."

Though the movie is good, my favorite part of the night is hearing Stasya laugh, watching her reactions, and having her in my arms.

"It's not a bad life, here with me, isn't it?" I ask while the credits roll.

"No. But sometimes I feel guilty being here." She gestures to the empty Pepsi bottles on the table and the VHS player. "Living like this."

"Why?"

"Don't you feel guilty having things that other people don't have? There are millions of people working day in and day out, staying away from trouble. Not out there breaking the law to get what they want." She looks down as if she's insulting me.

"Is that how you see me, Stasya? As someone who laughs when I see my comrades standing in line for bread? Do you think I enjoy seeing people suffer under a government who takes so much more than they give?"

She looks around my apartment. "I'm not saying you like it, but you're living the high life of the *nomenklatura*, not the life of your 'comrades.'" She curls her fingers into air quotes on the last word.

"I chose the path I did because I saw injustice and I didn't want to live under a system that oppresses its people and tells us it's for our own good. I want to be someone who incites change. If I have to break the law to do something about the inequalities across our country, I will. The people who are shaking things up to get freedom for all, are the ones who will go down in history."

"You think you will be in future history books?" she asks. "Lenin, Stalin, Khrushchev, Gorbachev—Antonov."

"I have big goals, Stasya. Big goals."

OUR BEDROOM ROUTINE HAS BEEN THE SAME EVERY NIGHT SINCE she arrived. She starts in her own bed and sneaks into mine sometime during the night. I'm not sure why she doesn't just get in my bed from the start, but I'm not complaining, since I've never slept as good as I do when she's in my arms.

"Can I ask you a question?" she whispers as she climbs into my bed, startling me out of a light sleep.

"Get some rest, Stasya." I close my eyes and yawn. "We'll have plenty of time to talk tomorrow."

"Kirya!" She elbows me.

My eyes pop open. "Geez!" I say, grabbing her arm and holding it down. "Yes, you can ask me a question. Ask me a million questions."

"Do you really think I belong to you?"

The question seems to be out of left field, but my answer will always be the same.

"Yes."

Her body stiffens and I feel anger heating up her skin. "You think I'm your property? Just because my father is an ignorant idiot?"

"I never said you were my property."

With an exasperated huff, she turns her body to face me. "You just said—"

"You asked if you belonged to me, and the answer is yes. You've been mine for years." I continue quickly before she flies off the handle. "Haven't you realized by now that I don't want to control you, Stasya? You are not a prisoner here. You're here because I can give you a better life than you ever dreamed of having."

"So, you think I belong to you because you give me things?" Her eyes are hard, but she's still in my bed. I don't blame her for venting her anger. If that's what she needs to do so she can move past this, I'll take whatever she has for me.

"No. It's all completely separate. I give you things to show that I can provide for you. Whether you realize it or not, I've always provided for you. I've always protected you."

"I do realize it. I'm not ungrateful." She looks away.

I place my palm on her cheek and bring her face to mine. "I've always wanted to give you everything, to make you happy however I was able. When I say you belong to me, it has nothing to do with money or power. I own your heart and soul. Someday you'll see the difference."

She wiggles out of my grasp and slides out of bed. "Maybe I will. Maybe someday I'll feel like any of this was a choice."

"I'm doing the best I can for you based on the choice your brother made, Stasya. In gaining freedom for himself, he turned his family into hostages."

She doesn't turn around, just slips out the door and shuffles to her room—or the couch—wherever the fuck she went.

I punch the pillow she'd been resting on, then grab it and squeeze it.

Why must I be blamed for Vanya's selfishness? He's the one who made the decision to go without her. She doesn't even know I had anything to do with it. And technically, the only reason I even got involved was because he trusted me. My negotiation and connections to get him out of the country helped as well.

The fact is: Leaving her behind was Vanya's decision. I didn't threaten him to go. I just helped.

I'm trying to do what I can to help her in a shitty situation, and I get anger and attitude.

Fuck it.

It's time to show her how her brother lives, so she stops being angry with me for trying to give her the best life I can.

I jump out of bed and rush to the living room where I left my briefcase. Hastily, not caring if I rip the pages, I pull out the latest edition of *The Hockey Paper*, a magazine that devoted an entire issue to Vanya.

There are multiple photos of his new apartment—on the top floor in a brand-new, high-rise that overlooks the Detroit River. He sits on a black leather couch, playing video games hooked up to a TV larger than any Russian has ever seen. There's another photo of him in the gorgeous red Corvette he drives to work, which is ridiculous and showy, since the arena is two blocks from his building.

Let her see how he lives and how he talks to the media. Let her see how he's having the best season any rookie has had in twenty years. Then, maybe it will sink in that her loving brother never mentioned taking her with him. He never mentioned sending her over after he was in America. He hasn't even tried to call her.

Out of sight, out of mind.

While she's safe in the arms of a criminal.

12

STASYA

*B*eing with Kirya over the last few weeks has been different in so many ways, but one of the things I find most unusual is that he and Slava drive almost everywhere. Must be a mafia thing, because Moscow has extremely efficient public transportation.

Though I take their beauty for granted now, when I was young, walking into a station felt like entering a museum. When we were bored, Vanya and I would get off at every stop just to see the gorgeous artwork. Some stations were like a history lesson, with brightly colored murals depicting the timeline of the USSR. They weren't the dirty, smelly, concrete caverns I'd heard about subway stations in other cities.

Truth be told, I'd always choose the metro because driving scares me. After having been on a waiting list for nine years, my entire family was excited when Papa finally received the call that there was a Zhiguli available. Though I'm not sure how much it cost, Papa drained our savings to buy it. It wasn't anything special, a drab, red box on wheels, but it was ours.

We barely had it for a year before the accident that killed Mama.

The main roads in Moscow are set up in a series of rings that start at the Kremlin and push out. Each ring was a wall at one time, protecting the Kremlin from invaders. Technically, we all understand the rings, but none of us, not even Papa, knew how to drive on them.

Many of the roads in the city are circular, twisting and turning without much ability to see what kind of traffic you're turning into. There may be another car coming—or worse—a bus, like the one that hit our car.

Mama died on impact, Papa suffered multiple lacerations on his face and chest and almost lost his right arm, and the car was destroyed.

So yeah, driving everywhere has taken some getting used to and Slava's aggressiveness doesn't help. The man is crazy behind the wheel. Every time he turns, I think we're going to be the next accident.

Today, he's driving us to the *Izmaylovo* District, a historical area in the eastern part of Moscow, just off the Moscow Automobile Ring Road, or MKAD. Despite its historical significance as the land belonging to the Romanov family, I've only ever been to this area one other time, years ago, when Vanya and I came to see a Lokomotiv football game. I don't remember there being any kind of market or stores around the stadium, but then again, we came in on the train, so I didn't see it from the motorway.

"What's that, Kirya?" I ask, pointing to the massive structure that looks like a marketplace—open on the sides and covered with a metal roof. There are hundreds of cars in the parking lot and hordes of people walking up to it.

"That's Cherkizovsky Market, Stasya. You are about to see *perestroika* in action," Kirya tells me with a laugh.

"We're going there?" I ask.

"Yes, Slava and I have work to do."

"What kind of work do you have here?"

He and Slava don't strike me as the type of men who sit behind a table, manning a booth at a market.

Kirya Antonov knows my deepest, darkest secrets—with the exception of my Dmitri Morozov mistake—it's only fitting I know some of his. Since I'm his "queen" now, asking shouldn't be off the table.

"I think you'll find observing is a better way to answer your question. Keep your eyes and ears open, and you will understand." Kirya pulls on black leather gloves and nods at my hands, which are folded in my lap. "Put your gloves on."

"It's not cold today," I say, puzzled at why I would put gloves on in July.

Kirya's eyes are as hard as his words. "Listen to me, Stasya."

I fold my arms across my chest. "Do you mean blindly follow your orders, like Slava and Igor?"

"I'm going to ask you to do things that you may not understand at first. But you will."

"Will I? Are you going to explain everything to me?"

"I promise you, I will."

It's not the answer I expect. So, instead of challenging him, I stuff my hands into the gloves and turn my gaze back to the window. We've pulled up in front of the market.

Kirya exits first, then takes my hand and helps me get out. As soon as my feet hit the pavement, Slava speeds off faster than he should in a crowd as large as this. Within seconds, we're engulfed in a sea of citizens—men, women, children—all headed toward the market.

"What did you mean about *perestroika* in action, Kirya?"

He moves closer, putting an arm across my shoulders to protect me from people pushing. It's a slight gesture, but it gives me warmth. Kirya is a man of his word. He cares about me and wants to protect me.

"This is what happens when a country restructures and allows private investors to rent government-owned spaces. It started as a physical education facility for Moscow State, but it's had a lot of uses over the last twenty years." His lips tickle my ear when he whispers, "Rumor has it, there's an underground bunker that was built for Stalin during the Great War. But I don't think it was ever used."

As soon as we enter, I'm speechless. Underneath the aluminum roof are booths and tables as far as the eye can see, each one overflowing with items no Soviet has ever been able to purchase in the GUM store. This place is filled with anything anyone could ever want.

I stop in the middle of the aisle to absorb everything, feeling my eyes getting wider with each new discovery.

Blue jeans. Brightly colored clothing in all shapes and sizes. Fur coats and boots. Toys and records.

"I feel like I've been transported to another world," I whisper.

It must have been loud enough for Kirya to hear, because he answers immediately. "You have," he says, leaning down again so I can hear over the hum of chatter. "Welcome to Cherkizon."

Someone bumps me hard and I turn around, ready to shout a few words. Whoever it was is already gone, lost in the sea of hungry shoppers.

Kirya moves his hand to my back and guides me forward. "This way."

"How could a place like this exist in Moscow without me ever seeing or hearing of it?" I ask him as we walk.

"Remember what I told you in the car? Opportunities present themselves when you have your eyes and ears open."

Indignation bubbles in my stomach. I'm not stupid. I know what's going on in the world.

Before I open my mouth, I catch myself. Kirya isn't calling me stupid. He's calling me naïve, which is something very different.

I've blindly followed the communist way because it's all I've ever known. Even over the last few years, when everything has gone to hell, I've kept faith in my country and its systems. If I ride the storm and stick to what I'd been taught, the Soviet Union would provide, like it has my entire life.

But Kirya is right. I *am* naïve. Staying in my pattern and pretending the Soviet ship wasn't sinking made me blind to what was going on around me.

"This is where you'll be selling your clothing someday."

I snap my head to him. "What clothing?"

"We have so much to discuss, Stasya. But right now, I have work to do. Come." He loops my arm with his and leads me down the aisle. "You can sit through my first meeting."

"Why can't I sit through all of your meetings? I thought you said you would tell me everything."

"Sometimes when people come to me, they want to be anonymous. They might be giving me information. They might feel unsafe because of threats from other groups. There are hundreds of reasons. They trust me to keep my word. And I don't plan on losing their trust. Do you understand?"

I nod.

"I will tell you anything you want to know, Stasya, but it's safer for all of us if you don't see the faces of those I'm telling you about."

It makes complete sense. And to be honest, I don't want to know any more than I have to. Which is why I haven't pushed him to tell me every detail about what he does.

The less I know, the safer I am.

We weave between booths, dodging men rolling large packages on metal dollies and women rifling through piles of scarves.

A large man in a black leather coat bumps my shoulder as we pass. When I look back, he's scowling, but bright red scars curve from the outside of his lips up to his jaw, making it look as if he's smiling from ear to ear. Without taking his eyes off me, he spits something on the ground.

I shudder involuntarily, stumbling as I shift my eyes straight ahead.

"Am I going too fast?" Kirya asks.

"Not fast enough," I mumble, craving more distance from the scowling man.

Kirya stops in front of a stairway. Just as he starts down, a rush of people run past us, knocking me against one of the tall, white shelving structures separating the booths. I'm not hurt, just surprised.

When I look toward the commotion, I see Slava grab a short, skinny man by his shirt collar and pull him close. He's snarling something I can't hear.

The man shakes his head, sneering at him and spitting something in broken Russian and a language I don't recognize. Slava raises a gun to the man's forehead.

No! He wouldn—

Brains and blood splatter across a wall of "I Love Moscow" sweatshirts.

I scream and grab onto Kirya, hiding my face in the nook between his body and arm. He puts his arm around me and ushers me down the stairs. Once at the bottom, he tightens his arms around me and holds me as I shiver.

"It's okay, Stasya," he whispers. "It's okay."

"What happened, Kirya?" I ask. "What was that?"

"Business."

I pull back. "Business?" I ask, my bottom lip trembling. "This is the business you came for? Why would you bring me to see that?"

Disgusted, I turn my back and fold my arms across my chest, hoping hugging myself helps soothes the shaking.

"That would have been you, Stasya." Kirya spins me around and pushes my back against the wall. His massive body heaves as he looms over me. "If Slava and I hadn't grabbed you before the men in that Vaz that was following you, you would be dead."

I meet his eyes. "You don't know that."

"I do!" He slams his palm on the wall, inches from my head, and I wince. "Last week, Sobakin's men kidnapped Evgeny Bobrov's mother. You know Zhenya, yes?"

I swallow the lump in my throat and nod. Of course I know Zhenya, my brother's teammate and friend.

"They gave him one day to pay. One day!" Kirya yells.

I flinch, turning my head from him. He grabs my jaw, squeezing it so I can't look away. Every time my chest rises, it hits his, a touch that might be comforting in another situation, but not here.

"She looked directly into their video camera and pleaded for her son to pay. Then they chopped off her head mid-sentence."

No. NoNoNoNoNoNo.

Vomit rises from my churning stomach and a tear slips down my face. I'd met Zhenya's mother at many hockey games. How could someone do that to her?

"I could never live with myself if that happened to you." He releases my chin and spins around.

As a million thoughts hit me at once, I slump against the wall and rub my cheeks with my hands.

It took me a while to process, but I saw the magazine Kirya left out for me a few weeks ago. The one that has pictures of Vanya's new, extravagant life. He's living in luxury and making no secret of it. If they didn't want to kidnap and hold me for ransom before then, I was definitely a goner once Sobakin saw that.

I've been thinking of Kirya as one of the bad guys, not realizing the heaviest things that weigh on his mind. Fearing for people he loves. Trying to keep them safe. And living with the regret of knowing some of them will still die.

I'm just about to reach out and touch his shoulder, but before I can, he says, "I have kept you safe this long and I intend spend the rest of my years protecting you. Now move."

UNDERNEATH THE MARKET IS A WORLD OF ITS OWN. WE PASS multiple doorways. Inside, a few look like bedrooms, with filthy mattresses and grimy blankets littering the ground.

Other rooms have tables lined with sewing machines and fabric rolls stacked to the ceiling. The grounds are dirty and disgusting, even for the city's standards. My stomach rolls with each room we pass.

I want to turn around, run up the stairs, and find the nearest metro station. There's no way I'm getting into Slava's car. Not after what I saw. I don't care if it's business or protection or what. I'm not part of this life. Murdering people isn't normal or acceptable—or something I'll ever get used to.

But I have no money, no way of leaving this place without Kirya or Slava. And even if I *could* leave, I'd never be able to find my way out.

"Pay attention, Stasya," Kirya commands. "If something ever goes down, you'll need to be able to get out of here."

The advice surprises me, but reinforces what he's been saying since day one. I'm a free woman. I can do what I want. He's trying to protect me when he wants me to be able to get out on my own.

"It's all so confusing," I mumble.

It's the understatement of the century. How could I ever find my way out of here? We've twisted and turned so many times through this underground maze, I don't even know which direction we came from.

"At first, yes, but you'll figure it out if you pay attention. You're smart, Stasya," he says, without looking back at me.

Flies hover above bodies sleeping on the floor. I stare hard, squinting to make sure I see the rise and fall of breath. The stench in the hallway smells like people haven't showered in days, maybe weeks.

Kirya stops in front of wooden double doors labeled with a small brass plate: *Chaynaya Komnata.*

A tearoom is the last thing I expected to see in the filthy underground of an illegal marketplace, but I suppose it makes sense. It's customary to meet over tea, so why would I think the mafia would be any different?

I'm completely stunned at the treasure behind the double doors. The Tearoom is small, but grand.

Igor sits at a booth facing the door, which, I've recently

learned, is a way of being vigilant. You can't see who's coming if your back is to the door.

I follow Kirya to the table, hovering behind him slightly.

A beautiful antique samovar sits on the edge while etched crystal glasses set in *podstakanniks* litter the table. There are two things directly in front of Igor: a gun and a mirror with a line of white powder. He leans down, holds one nostril, and snorts the powder into the other.

Though I haven't spent much time with him over the last two months, he makes me want to vomit. Hearing Kirya and Slava discuss keeping him away from me has me constantly vigilant.

"I've been holding down the meeting until you arrived." Igor sniffs and rubs his nose with the pad of his thumb before looking up.

Kirya looks around. There are a few other tables with patrons, but he doesn't seem to see the person he's expecting. "That doesn't bode well for you, considering he's not here."

When Kirya gestures for me to slide into the booth next to Igor, I fight to keep the disgust off my face.

"He had to piss." He shrugs. "Stasya!"

Up close, his stained teeth look even more yellow than they do from afar. His clothes reek of cigarette smoke and body odor.

"Please, call me Anastasiya," I say. The nerve of him to be so familiar with me.

"We'll be friends in no time." He pats my thigh.

I jump, scooting closer to Kirya, but before I say anything, Kirya's arm whips in front of my face and he presses his gun to Igor's forehead. I squeeze my eyes closed.

"The fuck, Antonov?" he asks, but doesn't move a muscle.

"Don't ever, ever touch her again," Kirya says calmly. "If you

SOPHIA HENRY

so much as brush her shoulder as she sits here, I will blow your motherfucking head off."

A man approaches our table and my stomach drops. Though his hair is shorter than I've ever seen it, I'd know those bouncing, brown curls anywhere.

Dmitri Morozov.

"Don't tell me he's the one who's supposed to keep me company later," I mutter to Kirya.

He lowers his arm and shoves the gun into the holster at his hip. "I thought you'd be happy to see an old...friend."

The way he pauses before the word "friend" makes me suspicious. There's no way Kirya knows what happened between Dima and me. It would have been impossible since he wasn't even at the New Year's party that night. He'd moved out of the apartment many years before and hadn't been back since his mother moved out—the same night he beat Papa.

"He is no friend of mine." I scowl. The last time I saw him was when he refused to help me. I'd walked miles to get to that training base and he sent me away like I was a dirty leper.

"So, you want to go to America?" Kirya asks as Dmitri sits in the chair across from us.

"It's the only reason I'd be here talking to you, Antonov." He glances at me, his face twisted in a look of disgust, as if I'm beneath him. It stirs up the rage inside.

"Is that any way to talk to the person who can help you get over there?" Kirya asks.

"The way I see it, you're going to get my money before I go, or after. I'm looking for the least violent route. Tell me the terms. I'll agree and be on my way," he demands.

"I vote for the violent route," I mutter under my breath.

Kirya snorts. "No love lost between you two is there?"

"There had to have been love in the first place for it to be lost," I say glaring at Dima.

"Why did you even bring her here?" Dima asks, shoving back in his chair and crossing his arms over his chest, as if he's annoyed. "If you're trying to mark your territory, you might as well piss on her."

Kirya jumps up, his hand flying to the gun at his side. "Watch your mouth, Morozov."

It's funny, Dima brought up the dog analogy, but he's the one averting his eyes and cowering like a bitch.

"You know," I say, looking up at Kirya who still looms over the table. "I don't know how you know, but you know. So let's put it aside and move on to the business at hand."

"Nothing gets by me, Stasya," Kirya reminds me as he lowers himself into his seat. He focuses his intense gaze on Dima. "Especially when someone disrespects you."

"I have nothing in my heart for him." My voice is strong because it's true.

Dima's jaw is stiff, his lips a firm line. If he feels anything for me, he doesn't show it. And that's fine.

Though there's no reason to hold hate in my heart for Dima anymore, I still haven't forgiven him for the way he treated me. It's still a fresh wound, but I'll let it go someday. I don't want something so trivial to eat away at my soul, and certainly not where he's concerned.

13

KIRYA

While Stasya showers, I put the finishing touches on her surprise. Ever since I saw the dress she made and heard how passionate she is about designing clothing, I've had an idea in my head.

I remove the sheet covering an antique, Imperial style secretary desk, which has been concealed since Slava and I carried it up last week. It matches the desk already in my office. Next to each other, they appear to be a set that may have been broken apart at one time, and now they're back together.

A reflection of Stasya and I.

I've been trying to make the apartment a space where she feels comfortable. Someday, I hope we'll sit in here working together, but until then, I want her to feel like she has a space of her own.

Pencils, crayons, scissors, various types of paper, and any other supplies she might need fill the drawers. I open each of them one more time to make sure everything's there, as if some supply-snatching troll came in and stole it all overnight.

When I hear the bathroom door open, I rush into the hall-way. "Hey!"

She jumps, then turns around. "Hi."

I wave her toward me. "Can you come in here for a minute?"

She glances at her bedroom door then at me. "Can it wait until I get dressed?"

"Yes. Yes, of course." I can't keep the disappointment from my voice. It's not an emergency, I'm just excited to see her reaction. There's no better feeling than making her happy.

Next thing I know, she's tiptoeing through the door, still wrapped in a fluffy white towel.

"Seemed important," she says with a nonchalant shrug.

My heart fills with pride, watching her eyelids open bigger when she catches sight of the new desk. She moves to it quickly and touches the top with her fingertips.

"You got a new desk!" she cries with excitement. "It's absolutely gorgeous."

"It's yours."

She looks up quickly. "What do you mean, it's mine?"

"Open the drawers." I nod encouragingly. She smiles as if she can't believe it and opens the top drawer on the right side—the one filled with pencils. She opens the rest, her grin growing larger with the discovery of each new treasure.

"After you told me you enjoyed designing clothes, I got this idea. You and Slava won't be able to sit at the park for long during the winter, so I wanted to give you a space to do it right here." I gesture around the room. "I'm picking up a sewing machine next week."

When she looks up, her eyes are glassy. "Kirya," she whispers, then puts a hand over her mouth. As she stares at the desk, a tear slides out and lands on the roll top. "Thank you so much. It's the most thoughtful thing anyone has ever done for me."

"It's the least I can do. I want you to feel at home here. If you're not happy, I'm not happy."

"Why is there a Russian-English dictionary in the bottom drawer?" She opens the drawer again, picks up the book, and starts flipping through the pages.

"We will embark on many adventures during our life together, Stasya. One of those adventures will be moving to America."

She looks up. "We're moving to the United States? That's the plan?"

"That's the plan," I confirm. "Do you remember when I met with Dmitri Morozov?"

"Ugh." Her face twists with disgust. "You were helping him get to the NHL, yes?"

"Yes. It's part of a new—legal—business Uncle Vitya and I just started. In the NHL, most athletes have someone to help them negotiate their contracts," I explain. "It's a called an agent. Since all of this is new for Soviets, it's opened up a brand-new business opportunity. Once I've gotten enough players over there, we can move there, too."

"Do you speak English?" she asks.

"*Yes*," I say in English, then switch back to Russian. "I speak fluently, so if you need help, just ask."

"You are a man of many secrets, Kirya."

"Not anymore, kitten. It was too difficult to keep the desk a secret. I want to share everything with you. If you ever want to know something, just ask."

She rushes to me and throws her arms around my neck. Having her in my arms, with her ear on my chest, feels right, like she was always meant to be there. She lifts her head and looks up into my eyes, and I'm lost.

Our chests seem to melt into each other, hearts beating as one as we stand, staring into each others eyes. I won't let go until she does. I'll never let go before she does.

14

STASYA

*E*ver since Kirya presented me with my own space to design, it's all I can think about. I probably spend way too much time in the office, but I have so many ideas rolling though my head, I feel like I'll forget them if I don't get them all down.

Despite wanting to spend as much time as possible with Kirya, it's been a bit hard to get used to being at Cherkizovsky's Tearoom and Discotheque two or three nights a week. It seems a bit excessive to me, but it's a huge part of Kirya and Slava's work, so I keep my mouth shut.

Within a few months, I've gone from a boring bank worker who rarely went out, to a mafia girlfriend, whose main social role is to be on Kirya's arm.

Though I never saw myself as someone's trophy girl, I must admit, playing the part is fun. It gives me reason to make new clothes and test new makeup—some of my favorite things.

At home, Kirya waits on me hand and foot, showing me how much he cares with acts of services or gifts he knows I'll like. The man bought me an antique desk and created an area for me to sit and sketch, for goodness sake. But when we're out, I understand my role is to serve him and I play it happily because I like being with him—so much it scares me.

Slipping back into friendship has been easy, like there wasn't a gap when we didn't see each other. It's refreshing be with someone who understands me. He knows who I was and who I've become.

There's one key difference between then and now—the intense sexual tension. It's scary and exciting.

Being with Kirya has given me confidence unlike I ever had. Some of that is due to the beautiful outfits I get to wear, but even more comes from the respect I receive as his girlfriend. Before being with Kirya, I didn't even want to acknowledge the mafia. Since being with him, I've had to learn a lot in a short amount of time—most importantly, structure and rank. As an *Avtoritet*, or captain, in the *Bratva*, Kirya leads a group of men and reports directly to a boss—in his case, his Uncle Viktor.

Learning his men was very important, as well, so I could decipher who was friend and who was foe—or who was higher level and who was lower. I learned very quickly that being an *Avtoritet's* girlfriend comes with perks and responsibility.

I'm treated with utmost respect, not like the dancers or the girls the men bring over to party with us for the night. And I'm responsible for keeping an eye on the girlfriends of Kirya's men, and talking to them if the need comes up.

Though we left the Tearoom fairy early tonight, we didn't come home alone. Slava, Drago—the guy he's tattooing—and a few girls they were talking to came as well.

It's almost two o'clock in the morning and I'm getting tired —and bored. The sound of Slava's tattoo machine has been grating on my nerves for the last hour, and there doesn't seem to be an end in sight. The spider crawling up Drago's neck looks so realistic, it's frightening. Which tells me all I need to know about Slava's talent.

As if reading my mind, he looks at me and nods to the spider. "When am I doing yours?"

I laugh. "If I got that spider on me, I'd scream every time I looked in the mirror."

"You're not getting a tattoo," Kirya says. His voice has the tone of finality, like it's the end of the conversation. It probably would be for one of his men, but he should know better with me.

"Yes, I am," I say, crossing my arms over my chest. "I made a promise, and I keep my promises."

Kirya stares at me, his eyes narrowing. "Who did you promise?"

"Slava."

"Fuck," Slava mutters, leaning closer to Drago. It looks like he would curl into the man's neck if he could.

"What kind of promise did you make Slava?"

"The very first day I was here, he tried to get me to go shopping for clothes like this." I pinch the clingy, black fabric riding up my thigh. "I told him I'd let him give me a tattoo if he took me to get pencils and notebooks instead."

He pinches my dress's thin strap. "I thought you made this?"

"I did! That was my point. Why would I waste money buying clothes that I can make?"

"Why?" He lowers his head to my ear and whispers, "Because you can." His lips move to my neck. "Because when you're with me, you don't have to make your own clothes anymore." Another kiss, this time on my shoulder. "Because I want to provide for you." His lips cover mine in an intoxicating kiss and my fingers slide into his hair.

When he pulls back, I'm dazed. "All I wanted was to sit in *Park Zaryad'ye* and sketch."

He laughs—a warm roar that coats me in happiness. "You are everything to me, Stasya. If making your own clothes and sketching in the park makes you happy, that's where Slava will take you."

I wiggle in his lap like a cheerful child.

"But there is only one man you should be making promises to—me."

Diffusing a jealous lover isn't something they taught in school, but I know what will bring him down. "Oh, I have many promises for you, Kirya," I say in my huskiest, sexiest voice, then whisper, "but they are for your ears only."

That gets me the exact reaction I want—Kirya's lips on mine again. One hand slides up my thigh and under my skirt while the other grips the back of my neck, holding my mouth to his. When his fingers enter me, I moan into his mouth. Both Slava and Drago whip around to see what's going on, but Kirya doesn't care. Nothing stops him from getting what he wants.

"Kirya," I say, twisting my hips and squeezing his fingers. He pulls his hand out from under my dress, leaving me wet and stimulated, and nowhere close to satisfied. He knows it. He puts his fingers in my mouth, urging me to taste myself.

"That's so fucking sexy, *kitten*. You drive me mad."

The girls start whispering. Despite having come with Slava and Drago, they've been competing for Kirya's attention since they arrived. It's almost as if they use his men to get to him. My backside has been glued to his lap the entire night, but it doesn't deter them. Hell, I've been glued to him for months now. But they don't care. They still try.

I'm not worried or jealous, because I trust Kirya. If he gave them attention that should be directed at me, it might be different, but he ignores them, whispering to me or talking to Slava instead. They're perfectly respectful women. I'm sure we'd get along in any other situation, but not when they're in my home in the wee hours of the night.

My pussy throbs, swollen and stimulated, and I need relief, even if I have to do it myself. I grind my backside into Kirya's lap before getting up. "I have to take care of this." His lips curl into a sinful smirk. "You coming?" I ask over my shoulder.

"No. And you won't be either." He reaches out and grabs my hips, sliding his hands up and down my thighs. "You will wait for me."

"Don't be long, okay?" The words come out in a breathy whisper.

"It'll only be a few more minutes." He leans forward and nips my hip with his teeth.

I nod and slowly make my way down the hallway where Kirya and I still have separate bedrooms. After getting undressed and washing off my thick makeup, I pull back the blanket on my bed. Before getting in, I hesitate and look at the wall that separates our rooms.

Why do I even pretend I'm not going to sneak into his bed, as I've done almost every night since I've been here?

At first, it was because I was afraid of being alone, but now, I can't stand not having his arms wrapped around me.

Tonight is different.

Tonight, I want him to find me in his bed—naked and ready for whatever he wants to do with me. Tonight, I will not fight my feelings for him. Tonight, he will be mine.

I'm ready to give every part of myself to Kirya.

Before, I was afraid of falling too deep into his lifestyle. How can I call myself a good person if I'm involved in this world of crime? Personally, I may not be killing anyone or breaking any laws, but I know it's happening. I'm interacting daily with the most prolific criminals in Moscow. I'm letting it happen, and I'm enjoying the benefits of the lifestyle.

And I'm not ashamed. Not when the country is letting its people go through hell. Everything we've ever known is falling apart in front of our eyes. Before meeting Kirya again, I was lucky if I could find butter and sugar in a store. Now, I can have butter and sugar from Italy if I want. I haven't had to stand in line for one thing since he rescued me.

Sometimes I feel guilty. Especially because I still have friends who feel the effects of communism every day. I've tried to help because basic food and consumer goods shouldn't be saved for a certain group of people and held from others.

One of the things I love and respect the most about Kirya is that he chose this lifestyle because he knew the way Soviet citizens have been treated under this system wasn't fair. It isn't right. He makes me want to be a better person—someone who can bring change and a better life for everyone—even if I don't always agree with their means to the end result.

I can't quite remember the moment when the fear fell away to a sense of power and authority. It makes more sense to take control than be a victim of my situation. If gangs want me because I have a rich brother in the NHL, I'm facing death no matter what I choose.

So, I choose to be happy.

* * *

KIRYA SLIDES IN NEXT TO ME, LIKE HE DOES EVERY NIGHT, BUT THIS time when he wraps his arms around me, his hand sweeps across my nipple. I feel his body stiffen, as if he's realized something's wrong. Then he brings his hand back to my breast and cups it gently, but doesn't grope or squeeze it.

"Stasya?" he whispers.

I flip over to face him, unable to keep the smile off my face.

"You realize you're naked in my bed, yes?" he asks. He looks more nervous than I've ever seen him.

"Yes." I nod and place my hands on his chest. His skin is warm. His heart pounds under my palms.

"Am I dreaming?"

"If you were dreaming, your pants would already be off," I tease, walking my fingers down to the waistband of his boxer shorts and curling them under the elastic.

He swallows. "Are you sure about this?"

I lift my hands to his face, sweeping my thumbs across his cheeks. "There is only one thing I've ever been sure of in my life —and that's you, Kirya."

Leaning closer, I softly press my lips to his. Without breaking the kiss, Kirya pushes me onto my back and climbs on top of me. He rubs his erection against me, letting me know he's ready for this moment as well.

My hands move to his boxers again, pushing them down the best I can with my fumbling reach. He holds himself up on one elbow, pushing one side down before doing the same on the other side. Once they're at his knees, I use my feet to push them all the way off.

"I promise I've done this before," he says with a laugh.

"Is this not how it is every time?" I ask. The fumbling was about the same with Dima, the only other person I've been with. Maybe that's how sex is supposed to be.

"Oh no, Stasya. I'm just nervous."

"Nervous?" I ask. "We've known each other forever, Kirya. There's no reason to be nervous around me."

He drops a kiss on my lips. "That's precisely why I am, *kitten.* I've been waiting for this moment for years."

Hearing him say that sends a chill through me. This beautiful, strong man, who can have anything and anyone, wants me.

He rises to his knees, giving me a full view of his excitement. "You're too good for me, Anastasiya."

"I'm not." I shake my head, dismissing his words.

He takes his cock in his hand and places it at my entrance, rubbing the tip in the wetness between my folds. "I need you to know how important you are to me, Stasya. I would never do this with you if you didn't possess my heart."

It's hard to focus on what he's saying, when I'm squeezing the muscles between my legs in fearful anticipation. Logically, I know the squeezing isn't closing any holes, but I'm so nervous at how I'm ever going to be able to accept him.

He enters me easily, which surprises me. I open my eyes to see his cock jutting out over my stomach. It's his hand between my legs, exploring me with his fingers. It feels so good, I relax and circle my hips, giving in to the pleasure. His fingers move up into me until he's pressing against me on the inside.

"Yes, Kirya!" I cry out.

After a few seconds, he removes his hand and grabs his cock, placing it at my entrance again.

I shake my head. "I don't think—"

He pushes in then pulls out quickly. My breathing speeds up. He does it again, pressing in further before pulling out. He does it over and over until I realize he's all the way in.

He thrusts gently, never coming too far out before sliding in again. The rhythm is exquisite. I wrap my arms around his torso, bringing him down on top of me. Soon, I'm rocking with him, enjoying the friction of our bodies rubbing together.

"You feel so good, Stasya. Just like heaven. I'm going to explode."

"Yes, Kirya, yes!" I cry out as my orgasm shatters, sending pulses of electricity through my body.

"Fuck!" Kirya roars, filling me with his release, before he's completely still for a moment. Then smooths a hand over my hair gently as he hovers over me, catching his breath.

His forehead falls to the pillow next to my ear. "We are one, Stasya. Connected for eternity from this point forward."

"We are a circle. No start. No beginning. There is no Stasya without Kirya."

All these years, how did I not realize my soulmate was right under my nose? Our lives have been intertwined since the day I was born.

15

STASYA

*M*y entire life, there was always one thing blocking me from being happy.

My father.

Which is why he's the last person I expected—or wanted—to see tonight at the Cherkizovsky discotheque while celebrating Slava's birthday.

The television rolls highlights of tonight's NHL games. My brother scored two more goals, bringing his total for the year to fifty-five. He's having the best season of his life.

I was having the best season of my life too, until Papa walked in.

The party is in full swing. The music is blaring. The birthday boy sits on a chair in the middle of the floor, getting a special dance from a stripper. And I'm on my boyfriend's lap, enjoying the ride as he fingers me under a table overflowing with food and vodka.

Kirya notices my "Ugh," which is a very different sound

than the "Mmmmm" of pleasure I've been humming for the last few minutes.

"It doesn't feel good, *kitten*? You want my tongue instead?" he whispers. Before I have a chance to answer, his gaze darts to the door. His eyes darken. "What the fuck is he doing here?"

I scramble off his lap and pull my dress down my thighs. He starts to stand, but I place my hand on his shoulder. "I'll handle him."

"Are you sure?" he asks, searching my eyes.

I nod and lean down to kiss his cheek. He straightens his suit coat and sits up in his chair. Always observing.

"Anastasiya!" Papa exclaims when I approach. He grabs my hands and pulls me to the side. "What are you doing here? This isn't a place for you."

My father, the number one person I feared most throughout my life, is worried about me being in an underground discotheque run by the Russian mafia. If it weren't so tragic, I may laugh.

"Well, ever since you lost me in a card game, I go where Kirya goes." My voice is firm, but I glance at my lover quickly. His eyes sear through me, but he lets me speak to my father without coming over.

Papa's gaze follows mine. His expression morphs from irritation to fear when he sees Kirya behind me, watching Papa's every move.

"That's not why you're with him and you know it, you stupid girl!" he whispers harshly.

"You're right about one of those things."

"Come home with me," he murmurs, changing his tone before someone notices how he's speaking to me. "Things will be back to how they were."

"What makes you think I have any desire to go back to how things were?"

"Don't act like your life was so bad, Stasya. You never went without."

"You're right. Thanks to *Babushka,* I never went without anything I needed." My fists clench at my sides as anger courses through my veins. He's so ignorant, he'll never see the truth about himself.

"You know what he does—who he is—and you still want to be with him?"

It's funny that he pretends to care about what Kirya does now that he doesn't benefit from it anymore. He never complained all the times his uncle brought home foods and treats that a regular Russian family would never be able to get. He had to have known Viktor Antonov was high-up in organized crime.

"I know exactly who he is and I'm grateful for everything he's done for me."

"You sold your soul to that devil. For what?" Papa growls. Purple veins bulge from his swollen, red nose. "Safety? If you think being with him is safe, you're stupider then I thought you were."

"You should watch yourself, Mikhail Grigorovich," I say in a sharp tone, having been insulted enough. A false sense of power from the connections I have behind me electrifies my blood. "You've been involved with Kirya's family for years. You enjoyed the benefits of everything they were able to provide."

"Who would have thought I would raise such a stupid girl." He scowls. "This gang is ruthless! They have no loyalty."

"Compared to whom?"

He leans back quickly, eyes bulging as if I'm crazy. "Compared to people like us."

"Us?" I laugh. "In all my years of knowing Kirya, he's never laid a hand on me." Papa's eyes flick to the scar above my left eyebrow where his ring dug into my skin when he punched me. "He *still* hasn't laid a hand on me. How does that compare to people like us. Or rather, people like *you*?"

As my father stares at me in silence, I notice how far downhill his health has gone since I saw him a few months ago. The same dark, hollow circles pool underneath his eyes, but his pale, ruddy skin is so bloated I barely recognize him. Losing his entire family within a few weeks of each other has taken a toll on him.

And still, I have no pity.

He must realize I'm not going to give him what he's searching for, because he shakes his head and sneers. "I was wrong, Anastasiya. Only a person with a soul has one to sell. You know mafia don't take wives, right? You are nothing but his whore."

"I suggest you take my advice and watch yourself," I whisper through clenched teeth. "You don't need another enemy."

I don't wish evil on my father anymore. But I can't lie and say I'm not pleased when I see the color drain from his face. With that thinly veiled threat, I pull back my shoulders and turn around abruptly, finished with this insane conversation.

Kirya watches intently, head tilted and eyes questioning as I approach. Slava is at his side, having abandoned his birthday dance when my father arrived. They both rise to greet me.

"Everything all right, Anastasiya?"

"Of course, Kirya." I lean forward and kiss his cheeks three times. He may love me—and I believe that to be true—but I don't know if he trusts me completely. He doesn't trust anyone completely.

Someday, that will change. I'm not sure what will make him realize I'm with him for the long haul, but someday he'll understand that my heart is true—and his. My heart has always been his.

Until then, I'll continue to sit at his left side.

"What have you done to her?" Papa shouts, running at Kirya. "You've turned my daughter against me!"

My breath catches in my throat.

Slava draws his gun, but Kirya waves him away. He steps back, but keeps a watchful eye on my father.

"You know what they say, 'a close neighbor is better than a distant relative,'" Kirya taunts him.

"Go to hell, you devil," my father snarls.

That's when I realize...he came here to die.

Papa would never pull the trigger on himself. He is a coward who needs someone to blame for his choices. Drinking himself to death must be taking too long. He knew if he came here and insulted me or Kirya—or anyone in this room—it would get him killed.

The shot comes from the back of the room and my father screams. He falls to his knees, clutching his arm.

"Papa!" It's an involuntary reaction. Even though I expected it, he's still my father and there was a part of me that didn't really think it would happen.

"What the fuck are you doing?" Kirya snaps at Igor, who runs up to him.

"You can't let him talk to you like that. He needed to be made an example of!" Igor yells, his breathing labored.

Kirya gets in his face, nose-to-nose with his newest soldier, teeth bared like a bear ready to attack. "I had it under control."

"You call that control? Allowing a piece of shit to yell at you in front of all these people?"

I remove my scarf and press it to the wound on my father's shoulder. Because of the angle, it would be impossible for me to wrap it tight enough to stop the bleeding. Either Igor has really bad aim or he only meant to scare Papa. My bet is on the former.

"I can handle a belligerent drunk calling me names. I'm not a child." He pushes Igor, who stumbles backward. "Go get someone to help."

"Fucking ridiculous," Igor mumbles, tucking his black shirt into his jeans as he stalks away.

Another gunshot erupts in my ear. My first instinct is to cower and bury my face in my father's neck. When I look up, I see Kirya, arm extended, Glock pointed at Igor, who's lying facedown on the concrete. Slowly, the man lifts his upper body up, as if he's a cobra trying to strike.

Kirya walks over and stands above him, placing the barrel between Igor's eyes. Drops of sweat slide from the wounded man's hairline to his brow.

"Was that a good enough example for you, cocksucker?" Kirya asks with a stony smile. "Slava! Find someone to clean these two up." He kicks Igor to the ground and quickly moves toward me.

I close my eyes, counting to ten silently as I wait for my heartbeat to slow.

"This is your life now," Papa whispers in my ear.

"Fuck you," I say, pressing my index finger into his wound and twisting it until he screams. Then, I get to my feet quickly, dropping him onto the ground.

Kirya raises an eyebrow, but I just smile sweetly.

I am his queen after all.

16

STASYA

$\mathcal{K}$irya grabs my hand, his eyes blazing with an intensity unlike anything I've seen. He pulls me away from the commotion and through a door behind the stage, where girls in sheer underwear have been dancing all night.

He doesn't speak, just drags me through the hallway so fast I have to jog to keep up with him. He pushes open another door and we're in the Tearoom.

I didn't even realize there was a secondary way to get in here, but of course there is. Multiple entrances and exits for multiple ways to escape.

I wonder if I went too far. Maybe I've ruined the innocent image he has of me when I was a naïve girl.

"Is everything okay?" I ask, but he's too busy talking to a waitress to have heard my question.

The woman nods and waves her hand, beckoning us to follow her before leading us to a small room. There's nothing in here but one, large high-back chair.

Though I don't know what's going on, the hair on the back of my neck stands up. Something I would normally chalk up to the short dress I'm wearing, but it's not the temperature. It's the feel of this room that has me spooked.

The woman leaves, but Kirya stays next the door. He doesn't take his eyes off me and he doesn't speak.

I'm getting nervous, but I'm trying not to fidget. Within a minute, the waitress is back, handing him a glass. He shuts the door and cranks the bolt.

"Kirya?" I whisper, unnerved by his gaze and silence. Did I do something wrong? Did I go too far?

As he moves toward me, I hold my breath, waiting to see what he's going to do. He stops in front of me, so close I can smell his sweat.

"What would you think of me if I told you that watching you inflict pain on your father got my cock hard?" he asks, grabbing my hand and brushing my palm over the front of his pants.

Pride fills my chest, not just because I've done something that makes him happy, but also because I've made him this excited.

What kind of person have I turned into? Where guns and blood make my pussy pulse. I blink and swallow the lump in my throat.

"It's sick, isn't it?" He grabs my other hand and places them both on his belt buckle. I understand the unspoken command.

My nervous fingers fumble at first, but I make quick work of it. Though he didn't say to, I unbutton his trousers and carefully lower the zipper. His massive cock drops out and I can feel the wetness pool between my legs.

"We're going to have to do something about this, Stasya." He steps away from me and moves to the chair, dropping into it as if he's the king of the castle. Maybe he is. I have no clue if he has ownership in the market or not.

He rolls the vodka in his glass with a slight twist of his wrist, watching me intently through half-closed lids. His legs are open, feet firmly on the floor. Cock on display.

"Dance for me, Stasya."

"What?" I ask, puzzled at the odd request. I'm ready to drop to my knees and suck him off.

"Dance. For. Me."

"I'm not a good dancer," I dismiss him. I love to dance, but despite multiple trips to discotheques after work with girl-friends, I'd never gotten very good at it.

"That's a lie. You've always been a beautiful dancer. Even back when we were kids. While all of us kids were stomping through flowers, playing war with tree branches as guns, you were dancing."

"I was a silly child." I shake my head, dropping my gaze to the floor.

"You've mistaken my command for a request, Anastasiya. I'll only allow that once."

Sometimes I forget I'm a prisoner of circumstances. No matter how much I love him, he won't let me walk out the door. He would hunt me down and take me again.

All in the name of my own safety.

I don't know what to do, but disrespecting him isn't an option, so I start spinning around like I did when I was a child, arms out like propellers. I'm standing on my toes and using one foot to turn myself in small, quick circles.

The euphoric action reminds me of warm Moscow summers, playing in *Alexandrovsky* Garden, back when life was simple, stable, and I had nothing to worry about. Just thinking about those days makes my heart light. The only thing missing is the sweet and spicy scent of pansies and lilacs swirling around me.

When I catch Kirya's eyes, his jaw is tight and his eyes are glassy as he stares at me. "That's not the dancing I want." He lifts his cock and starts sliding his hand up and down.

My arms drop to my sides, the momentary joy extinguished by his rejection. Despite being a fairly confident person, he makes me feel like a wet chicken. My spirits deflate as I think about how ridiculous I'll look dancing for him compared to the beautiful, lithe dancers we saw in the next room.

"I don't know how to dance the way you want me to. Maybe I should fetch a girl from the disco." I wave my hand toward the door. "One of the ones dancing on the tiny platforms with no clothes on."

"If I wanted one of those girls, they would be here. I only want you, *kotyonok*." He leans forward, sets his glass on the floor, then points to the empty space between his open legs. "I want you right here in front of me, grinding your pussy against my face. Now."

The lust swirling in his eyes eases my insecurity.

I hurry toward him because I don't want him getting any more frustrated with me. And I want his mouth between my legs. I crave his tongue and fingers inside of me.

When I'm in front of him, I shake my hips, willing myself to pretend there's music, which is just as difficult as I thought it would be. I feel like a fool, but I don't want to disappoint him. On the contrary, the only thing I want is to please this man.

After a few more jerky hip movements, he grabs my thighs and presses his face between my legs, inhaling me. "Stasya," he moans, inching my skirt up.

Instead of letting him, I start circling my hips slowly, dancing like he asked me to. His nose rubs between my legs, creating a sweet friction. He tries to stop me, but I wiggle out of his grasp.

"Oh no, Kirya! You wanted a dance," I remind him, teasingly swatting his hand away when he tries to touch me again. "You will get a dance."

He could grab me and hold me still if he wanted, but he doesn't. Instead, he reaches over to retrieve his glass from the floor and falls back into his oversized chair, watching me intently with an amused smile on his face.

"This better be good, Stasya, or there will be consequences." His smile is wicked—a preview of what's to come.

My lips twitch, trying to keep my composure. Something tells me I'll like the consequences.

It's only him and I in this room, so I can do anything. Instead of dance, I move closer, then lift my skirt to give myself room to maneuver, placing my knees on either side of him. When my thigh presses against the gun on his hip, I look down and a ridiculous idea pops into my head.

My heart pounds, nervous, but unashamed at what I'm about to do.

Kirya watches me intently as I slide my hands across his thigh toward the gun. He tilts his head with interest. Despite my fear, I lift the Glock from the holster and hold it gingerly between us.

I can't even believe I know the difference between the Glock and the *Stechkin*.

"Stasya," Kirya says slowly, as if he's easing me off a cliff. "Please give that to me."

I know enough to point the barrel toward the wall. "Do you know what I want you to do with it?" I ask.

He shakes his head and swallows hard.

I catch his eyes, then turn the handle to him. He takes it

from me. I lick my lips and move my gaze from the gun to the throbbing area between my legs. His eyes widen.

"You're not serious," Kirya says, shaking his head. Beads of perspiration line his upper lip.

In answer, I grab his cock and rub it against my pussy so he can feel how wet and ready I am.

"Fuck," he hisses, closing his eyes. "This is fucking insane."

Leaning in, I brush his lips with mine and dare him with a whisper. "Do it."

I'm not expecting the force at which he ravishes my mouth. His tongue lashes mine. His lips are hard, almost bruising.

When he pulls back, I'm breathing heavy, my breasts bouncing in his face as I heave on his lap, coating him with wetness.

I lift up, and he obliges my depraved request, sliding the barrel over my slit.

"Yesssss," I moan, letting my eyelids flutter closed as I rub against it. The metal is hard, yet warm from our hands.

He watches my reaction as he does it again, only this time, he pushes the barrel into me. I buck forward, my chest hitting his chin. My eyes roll to the back of my head and excitement blasts in my core. He slides the barrel in and out, flicking my clit with his thumb. The pressure on the swollen, sensitive part between my legs is too much and not enough at the same time.

I grab his hair, squeezing it in my fists, and scream out, "Oh my god, Kirya!"

Suddenly, the gun hits the floor. He grabs my hips and fills me with something much thicker. He thrusts in and out, faster and faster, pounding my pussy with his engorged cock while rubbing circles over my clit.

I've never seen him so feral, so completely unrestrained, as he is right now, fucking me on his throne. Suddenly, there's a shift in the air and everything blurs.

Power. Sex. Love. Passion. Danger.

Electricity buzzes through my veins, alive with the knowledge I bring him this much pleasure.

When he explodes inside me, it's so intense I can barely breathe. He buries his face in my neck. "You will be the death of me, Stasya. And I will die with a smile on my face."

17

KIRYA

"I chose to be with you, Kirya. That means I accepted this life and everything that comes with it. We are equals, yes?" Stasya asks, dropping an earring onto the silver tray on her dresser. "I'm not talking about being on your level in your organization. I don't want anything to do with your business. But I will not be treated as a prisoner. Not if you really want me in your life as a lover and partner."

"When have I ever treated you as a prisoner?" I ask.

"Unless I'm within these walls, I'm never alone!" She sets the second earring on the tray and throws up her arms. Her feet slide across the wood floors as she strides to the window. "I can't even take a walk without Slava lurking behind me."

"It's for your protection, Stasya. Not because you are a prisoner," I explain, for what feels like the millionth time. "Do you understand how devastated I'd be if something happened to you?"

She silently stares out the window of our bedroom,

observing whatever's happening below on *Gorky Ulitsa*. I continue, "I couldn't go on. I'd put the *Stechkin* to my temple and fire it."

No answer. I tell her I'd kill myself if anything happened to her and she doesn't answer.

"Jesus!" I pull my hair sharply. "Sometimes I think I need to fuck some sense into you."

She scowls at me. "Fucking doesn't change anything."

That's where she's wrong. I cross the room quickly, grabbing her shoulders, and lifting her to her feet.

"It does," I say, staring into her blazing eyes. My cock swells with every heavy breath she takes. "Every time I take you, another piece of the invisible wall you have up dissolves away. I own you with every kiss and every thrust. I own your heart. Your soul. Your pussy."

Her hair is straight today, different from her usual big bouncy, hair-sprayed curls. It feels smooth as satin as I slide my fingers through it. My fist closes at the roots and I tilt her head back. She gasps, then tightens her jaw defiantly.

"You like being owned, Stasya. I can tell by the way your nails dig into my back when I'm fucking you. I can tell by the way you scream my name when I go harder. If you didn't like being mine, you wouldn't be wet and ready to accept me every time I touch you. You can say no, but you don't."

"Can I?" she asks. "Can I really say no?"

Round and round we go. She knows how much I love her. She knows I'd jump in front of a bullet to keep her safe. If it makes her feel better to rage at me every time she feels out of control, I can talk her down from the ledge.

"Sobakin knows I control Vanya, so the threat to your safety is probably over. If you're only here because you think I'm holding you captive, go." I release her abruptly, step back, and point to the door. "I want you to be here because you see yourself by my side forever. But if you choose to leave, don't curse my name if you get kidnapped."

"There you go with your guilt trips and threats, Kirya." She mimics my voice. "'Go on, leave me, but you'll get killed if you do.' You keep reminding me that I have no choice!"

"I have no threats for you, Stasya, just truth. I'll always keep an eye out for you because I love you. I thought you knew that. I thought you could see that in every fucking thing I do to make your life better. If you're looking for someone to beg you to stay, I'm not that man. I don't beg. I command."

She's silent for a minute, her lips and chest heaving as she contemplates her next move.

"What's your command for me this time, big pine? If you own me, what do you want from me right now?"

This is why I love this woman. Sometimes I think she likes angry sex more than any other mood. I have no complaints if she wants to vent her grievances then seamlessly move from fight to fuck.

"Suck me," I say, quickly unbuttoning my jeans and freeing my erection.

She doesn't hesitate, dropping to her knees and taking my cock in her tiny hand.

Every time she takes me in her mouth, I feel like I could come within seconds, but I've gotten really good at holding off. The longer I get to feel her mouth and hands on my dick, the better. I brush her hair out of her face so I can see her eyes while she swallows me. When I start to come, she directs me into her mouth. I close my eyes, allowing her to control me as I jerk and spasm.

When I finally open my eyes, I swear I'm the luckiest man on earth. The most gorgeous woman kneels between my legs with my cock in her hand and cum dripping from her chin.

"You taste so good it's as if enjoying you is a sin. I shouldn't like it, but I do," she says, licking her lips.

"I taste like sin. That has to be one of the best compliments I've ever been given." I pull her to her feet and rush her to our bed. I climb over her, lean down, and lick my juices off her face.

Her eyes sparkle as she laughs. "How do you do it, Kirya? How are you both angel and devil? Good and evil? Saint and sinner?"

"'Every saint has a past, and every sinner has a future.'" The quote explains me perfectly. Trying to do the most good for others led me to a lawless life. The criminal on the outside doesn't define who I am inside.

She tilts her head. "Did you just make that up?"

"No! It's a famous quote. Oscar Wilde."

She covers my mouth with her hand and looks around the room with wide eyes, paranoid that someone will burst in at any moment. "You mustn't speak like that, Kirya. The walls have ears," she whispers. "If they hear you quoting non-Soviet authors, you'll be sent to the gulag."

I lick her palm and she immediately pulls back in repulsion, frowning as she wipes it on my shoulder. I laugh and tickle her. "Why the look of disgust, Stasya? I thought you liked my tongue."

She smiles like she has a secret. Or maybe it's her way of protecting the last layer of modesty because she likes all the things I do to her with my tongue. Either way, I'm about to test my theory.

I roll her onto her back and lift her nightgown, taking a

moment to appreciate the smooth, fair skin of her lithe body. When I take hold of her waist, she lifts her pelvis toward my face, beckoning me to taste her. I press my lips to her stomach, kissing the soft skin above her belly button.

"Where is that tongue, Kirya? The one that barks orders and quotes classic literature in the same breath." Her stomach presses against my lips every time it rises. I inhale her sweet lavender scent.

"I'm multi-dimensional," I tease, lifting her legs over my shoulders. "Just like you." I stop to kiss the inside of her thigh. "You are so sweet and kind." I slide my hands from her waist, under her ass. She lifts ever so slightly, her wet pussy gliding across my chin. "But you like the power you have at my side. You like being different—special."

Despite the divine scent that makes me want to dive right in, I turn my head and lightly bite her other thigh. She cries out softly and squeezes my face between her legs, putting my mouth directly where she wants it.

"Everyone likes feeling special." She gasps.

"That's true. But it's especially true for you because no one has ever made you feel that way, have they?" Holding her open, I lick her folds slowly, before swirling my tongue around her clit. "You never got any attention."

"You gave me attention," she whispers, watching me intently. "You always made me feel special, like I was worth something."

"You are worth something. You are worth more than a million Fabergé eggs."

It's the last thing I say before plunging my fingers into her and flicking her clit with my tongue. I'll never get tired of making her moan with pleasure.

Afterwards, Stasya lays on my chest, exhausted and satis-fied. My eyelids droop, ready to plunge into dreamland.

"You're not a sinner, my love," Stasya whispers. "People may judge you harshly or be afraid of you, but I know the truth. I know the good inside you." She places her hand on my chest, directly over my heart. "Everything you do is to make life better for others. I know that above anyone."

18

STASYA

*A*fter months of paying attention, I'm finally comfortable weaving through Cherkizovsky's underground. Though, Slava is still at my side, pulling me right or left, steering me away from things I shouldn't see. And I appreciate it.

People who say knowledge is power, were never part of the mafia.

Today, I'm lucky enough to stroll the halls on Kirya's arm. He's been so busy bringing on new hockey clients, I rarely see him during the day, but he cleared his lunch hour because he had a surprise for me.

"Are you ready?" he asks with a sparkle in his eyes.

"Yes!" I clap my hands together, wondering what could possibly be behind the door that has him so excited. The market itself is booming, but underneath is a sad place—a third world country of its own. The only consolation I have is that it provides money, food, and shelter for the thousands of people who work here.

As he opens the door slowly, I lean forward, hoping to catch a glimpse of something.

Tables lined with sewing machines make up the front half of the room. At each machine, there's a person hunched over, working diligently. Not one head lifts when the door opens and Kirya and I walk in.

I move through the room, past the machine tables. At the next station there's a women hand-sewing individual garments. Along the back wall are reams of fabric stacked to the ceiling, in every color and texture imaginable.

"Welcome to the place where your clothing will be made," Kirya says. "For now. Once your line gets off the ground, we'll have to have a warehouse, of course."

"Wait? Are they really working on my designs, Kirya?" I ask, stopping to peer over a woman's shoulder. She's sewing crystals onto the pockets of a denim skirt I designed.

My hands fly up to cover my mouth and I spin around, watching the people working. That's when I spot the racks. I dash over to them and grab the first piece I reach.

It's one of the first dresses I ever put on paper.

"Will that be Anastasiya Antonova's signature piece?"

"That's not my name."

"Not yet."

The thought of being his wife makes me absolutely giddy.

"My favorite part about sharing an office with you is watching you work, Stasya. I see the passion you have for your drawings, the designs. I heard you and Svetlana talking on the phone a few weeks ago. When she said multiple people complimented her on the pieces you made her and wanted to know where she got them. And it gave me this brilliant idea."

"To sell my clothes?"

"Absolutely!" he replies. "You will be a business owner."

"Kirya, I appreciate this so much," I begin, choosing my words carefully so I don't sound ungrateful, "but you know that I don't want to be involved in this illegal market."

"I know, kitten, but it's a good place to begin. And it will give you the business experience you'll need to open a store in New York."

"New York? You're just teasing me now!"

"I'd never tease you about such an important dream, Stasya," he says earnestly. "But I won't force you either. If this isn't something you want, just let me know and I'll let it go. You can do it for fun, or for yourself and friends."

"Of course I want this! I want a store in New York and I want to have my clothes available all over the world!"

He looks at me with reverence. "There's only one thing I want in this world."

"What's that?"

"To see you happy."

Warmth floods my cheeks. I'll never take his compliments and kindness for granted.

He slides his hand over my head and through my hair, before cupping me behind the ear. "You are my rock, Stasya. Together, we are changing lives of Russians for the better."

Kirya is the most generous man I've ever known. Always thinking of others before himself.

When I first thought about the choice he gave me, I was confused. I understood his duty to protect me, but him wanting me for more blew my mind. He could have any woman in Moscow, why in the world would he choose me? He never gave me any indication he liked me in any way other than someone who was like family to him. Or maybe he did, and I was too thick to see it.

"I think you want more than that from me," I tease, fingers crawling up his chest.

He wraps his arms around me and pulls me close. "Oh, that's not a want, my love, that's a *need*."

19

KIRYA

Stasya's been working long hours, creating new designs, overseeing the production of her clothes, and building her inventory before she opens her booth at the market. Because there's still so much to do before it will be ready, I didn't think she would agree to take a break.

Thankfully, she's smart enough to know the rest will rejuvenate her for the hard work ahead.

"This is our stop," I say as we approach Peredelkino Station.

She scoots closer to the edge of her seat, waiting impatiently for the *electrichka* to come to a complete stop. She's been glowing ever since I told her I was whisking her away for an overnight trip to the country.

It's a much-needed break from the city for both of us. As much as quiet time to connect with Stasya excites me, I'm even more excited for the surprise I have for her.

"If you move one more inch, you'll be on the floor," I tease, pinching the denim covering her outer thigh. She glances at me with a bright smile that reminds me of when she was a girl—

carefree and happy. Back in the days when Vanya was always home and her father directed most of his alcohol-induced anger toward her mother.

She's finally wearing the blue jeans I bought her a few weeks ago. After her initial shock at seeing the price tag, she refused to wear them, claiming I spent far too much money. She argued she could get six pairs for the same price at Cherkizovsky. The girl who thought jeans that cost me over one hundred American dollars were too casual for the city saved them for this trip, to milk goats and chase chickens.

Maybe she's trying to prove a point. A hundred dollars is expensive for something you wear on a farm.

I don't give a fuck what she wears—expensive jeans to milk goats, fur coats to ride a horse. She's worth every single penny I spend on her. Maybe someday she'll realize that. Maybe she'll realize she doesn't have to live the Soviet way anymore.

I can't expect her to change overnight. The mindset is so ingrained, it's even hard for me to shake, and I was raised to rebel against communism.

Which tells me everything I need to know about her. She is the same wonderful, kind-hearted soul I've always known. She is not a money-hungry woman, looking for someone to provide for her. Though, I wouldn't blame her if she were. I don't blame one person here for wanting things we've been deprived of for so long.

If Stasya told me she wanted to take a bath in diamonds, I'd make it happen.

I slide my hand through her long, blonde hair, until my fingers brush her white button-down shirt. There are faint brown spots scattered across the collar.

"Is this mine?" I ask, brushing my thumb over the stain.

She turns to face me quickly, inadvertently knocking my

hand away. "Oh, Kirya, I'm sorry, I didn't ask." Her words gush out, as if she's afraid of my reaction. "You have ten identical shirts in your closet, so I didn't think you'd mind." She plucks the fabric at her chest and holds it out. "I even took one that was old and stained, just in case."

Taking her chin between my thumb and forefinger, I lift her face. "Shhh, kitten, it's okay. I'm not mad."

"Are you sure? I—"

"The last time I saw you in that shirt, I was making you breakfast after I fucked you raw. So, no, I'm not mad." I look at my lap where my dick swells under my jeans, and her eyes follow. A small smile lifts her lips when she sees how excited I am at seeing her in the shirt she loves to wrap herself in after sex.

I don't have the heart to tell her the stains on the collar are splatters of blood. She's already seen violent parts of my life, so there's no need to bring up stories that will repulse her—especially here, when we're trying to relax.

For someone who didn't even want to wear jeans at first, they've become a staple in her signature casual look. Her classic beauty makes her look like a model plucked from an American fashion magazine.

As we walk, Stasya inhales deeply. "Don't you love the air here, Kirya?"

"I do."

"I feel like I can breathe a little easier here. Maybe it's the extra oxygen, or maybe it's because I feel my happiest when I'm in nature. Though I love living in the city, summers at our *dacha* were some of my favorite memories. Warm wind in my hair, swimming in Pioneer Lake."

Her thoughts trail off as we approach a green, two-story

house with a bright yellow door. She glances at me, then back to the door. "Whose house is this?" she asks quietly.

"Knock and find out." I nod, encouraging her.

She taps lightly, as if she's worried about disturbing someone.

"I'll be honest, Stasya, I could barely hear that and I'm standing right next to you," I tease, nudging her shoulder with mine. "You think someone is this mansion is going to hear that?"

She sticks her tongue out at me, then knocks again—much harder this time.

"Calm down! I heard you the first time!" comes a voice from inside.

Stasya's eyes widen and she looks at me with surprise.

When the door swings open, Olga Kravtsova steps out, ready to curse at the annoying knocker.

"*Babushka*?" Stasya cries, eyes wide in disbelief.

"Anastasiya! My Anastasiya!" The old woman greets her, kissing her three times before throwing her arms around her.

Tears pool in Stasya's eyes. Pride fills my chest. Over the last few months, I've been the source of so many of her tears, when all I ever wanted was to make her happy.

When the women finish their embrace, Olga steps back, wiping her eyes with the back of her hand. "I've been wondering when this lug would bring you to visit me."

She throws me the familiar evil eye, a look she's given me countless times. Just thinking about it brings a smile to my face.

I still remember when Vanya and I would sneak into the kitchen, hoping to steal a piece of still-warm, fresh baked bread. She'd give us the look before slapping our knuckles with a wooden spoon.

"What are you smiling for?" Olga asks. "What's funny?"

Stasya covers her laugh with a cough, but composes herself quickly to save me from Olga's wrath. She latches onto the old woman's arm and guides her through the doorway. "Forget him, *Babulya*. We have so much to catch up on. How have you been? Tell me everything."

Instead of following, I take our bag to one of the bedrooms.

This *dacha* is not the same one where Stasya and Vanya spent their childhood summers, which is why she was so surprised to see who was behind the door.

When I moved Olga out of Moscow, Vanya pleaded with me to set her up somewhere she would love. Knowing she would never agree to move to America, he wanted her to ride out the rest of her years living better than she ever had.

Safety was my number one concern, as the Kravtsov family was still being pursued by the KGB and Sobakin's men at the time I moved her. The safest place I could think of was Peredelkino, the quiet village tucked away in a pine forest thirty minutes outside of Moscow. It's known as a writer's colony because so many great Russian authors have lived here—Boris Pasternak, Bella Akhmadulina, Andrei Voznesensky. Writing without fear of imprisonment is much easier to do when living away from the influence of the government.

My uncle bought this giant, colorful house fifteen years ago for his parents to live in. Unfortunately, they were only able to enjoy it for a few years before they passed. It had been empty until I moved Olga there.

At first, I offered to move her to the United States, to live in New York with my mother and uncle. I wasn't sure if she would enjoy living in solitude at the *dacha*. I had no doubt she could take care of herself, but she had lived her entire life under the Soviet system. For some, living alone with the nearest neighbor down the road, rather than in the next room, can be a difficult adjustment.

But she refused to go to America. She chose the country and seems to love it. She took to gardening straight away and even bought some goats and chickens.

I didn't expect it, but I can't say I'm surprised. Though Olga is much more gruff, she and Stasya are very similar. They're both smart, strong, hard-working, and able to take care of themselves. And neither woman is afraid to stand up to me.

20

STASYA

After visiting with *Babushka*, Kirya and I spend the afternoon foraging for mushrooms, though it's the end of season, so we're not able to find many.

I'm bent over, looking near a tree, when I hear a shrill voice behind me.

"Look out! It's Baba Yaga!" Kirya yells, running toward me. At first, I think he's coming to save me from the wicked witch of Russian folklore, but as he gets closer, I notice the devious smile on his face and long stick in his hand, and realize he's playing Yaga's part.

I scream with fake terror and take off running, but I'm no match for his speed. He catches me within seconds, dropping the stick before wrapping his arms around me and pressing his teeth against my neck. He tackles me to the dirt and kisses my neck where his teeth nipped. His mouth moves up, kissing my chin and cheeks and, finally, my lips.

His mouth is soft and gentle. When he lifts it from mine, he says, "I love you, Stasya. I always have."

His words conjure a memory I hadn't thought of in forever. A picnic in a park where Kirya hinted at how he felt about me. In my head, I see it clear as day.

"WHAT ARE YOU DOING HERE?" I ASK, SURPRISED TO SEE KIRYA. HE hasn't hung out with us in months—maybe even a year.

"Am I not invited to picnics anymore?"

"Why would you want to be?" I ask. "Aren't you too old and cool to hang out with us?"

"Too old to eat with my family?" he teases, dropping onto the grass next to me. "Never!"

"Family?" I glare at him. "Family doesn't disappear for months and show up at park, looking for food."

"Actually, that's exactly what family does." He laughs and reaches for the basket. I slap his hand and he draws back quickly. "Geez, Stasya. I didn't realize my absence weighed on you so heavily."

It did, but I won't admit that to him. I could never tell him how much I miss seeing him in the hallways, or when he would pop in to watch What? Where? When? *with us.*

I burn for him and he thinks of me as a sister. A meek girl he has to protect. He's probably got a girlfriend at university with fashionable bleached-blonde hair, who smokes the luxury cigarettes he buys off foreigners.

"You can trade all that stuff you buy from tourists for much better things to eat than the beet sandwiches I packed."

"Beet sandwiches?" Kirya asks, turning up his nose slightly as he peers into the basket.

"It's all we had," I tell him indignantly, then continue in a quieter voice, "Papa didn't make it to the store."

"How do you and Olga keep the faith?" His gaze catches mine

before I avert my eyes to my lap. He pats my knee playfully. "I'm sure the sandwiches are delicious. May I have one?"

I look over my shoulder to the bench where my brother sits with his face plastered to Elena Petrova's and shrug, handing Kirya the sandwich wrapped with yesterday's Pravda. "You can have Vanya's."

Kirya laughs and accepts without hesitation. He slowly unwraps the newspaper and sniffs the food.

"Enough of that, Kirya!" I kick his foot lightly. "It's vinegret on Babushka's homemade bread."

Without delay, he takes a gigantic bite. As he chews, he sighs and his eyes roll back with delight. Once he's swallowed, he says, "Even cardboard would taste good on Olga's rye bread."

"But what do you think of the beet salad?" I look up at him, hoping my question doesn't sound too desperate.

Even though I haven't seen Kirya in months, I've fallen right back into the pattern of wanting to please him. Wanting him to notice me as something other than the pathetic little girl who needs to be consoled after her father's violent temper erupts.

I'm not that little girl anymore. I'm not weak or helpless.

Last night, when Papa came home with four bottles of vodka, rather than the food he was supposed to bring from the store, I didn't cry or get upset. Instead, I created an entire meal out of ingredients we had in the kitchen.

I've been cooking more often recently, trying to take some of the work off Babushka. Though she tells me she would wither and die of boredom if she didn't have washing and cooking to do, I still want to help her.

Kirya takes another bite and pauses to chew before finally saying, "It's one of the best things I've ever tasted."

His compliment brings warmth to my cheeks. I raise my sandwich to hide my smile.

"Then again," he adds quietly, "I haven't tasted everything I want to."

My heart races when his full pink lips raise in a sexy smile. He stares at me, his dreamy eyes bright as he waits for my reaction. I move toward him as if an imaginary string connects our hearts.

"Is that my sandwich?" Vanya asks, jolting me out of my lust-induced fog.

"Yes," Kirya and I answer in unison, inching away from each other.

"Well, that's a shitty way to treat your brother while he's home from the military," Vanya says.

"You play hockey." Kirya balls up the newspaper and throws it at Vanya. "You're not on the front lines of war."

"I thought maybe you'd had enough to eat. You must have gotten some of Elena's lunch with how far your tongue was down her throat," I tell him dryly.

Kirya chokes, hacking on his sandwich. I slap his back until he holds up a hand. Tears slide out of the sides of his eyes. He grabs my drink and starts guzzling.

"It wasn't that funny," Vanya says, stalking away from us.

Kirya cough-laughs a few times, then says, "It was."

One of the things I love most about being with him is that no matter how long it's been since we last spoke, we pick right back up where we left off. Banter, silliness, teasing Vanya. He's always been one of my favorite people to be with.

The wind rustles his hair, which is longer than I've ever seen it. Dusk will descend soon, bringing colder air with it. I didn't bring a jacket because I didn't think I'd be here for this long.

"I don't want to keep you, Kirya. I know you're busy these days." Hastily, I start packing up the picnic.

"Spending time with you outshines anything I ever have going on."

. . .

KIRYA'S VOICE PULLS ME OUT OF THE MEMORY. "THERE'S A Pushkin poem I haven't stopped thinking about ever since we reconnected," he says, lying back and folding his hands under his head. A small smile plays on his lips as he gazes into the distance.

"Really?" I ask. "Which one?"

He turns his head to me and begins,

> *"I loved you; and perhaps I love you still,*
> *The flame, perhaps, is not extinguished; yet*
> *It burns so quietly within my soul,*
> *No longer should you feel distressed by it."*

I'm sure most people don't think of Russians as romantic, but we all know literature by heart. We can recite Tolstoy and Pushkin at the drop of a hat. Hearing him recite one of the most famous love poems to me brings tears my eyes. It's a very special moment when the man you've loved since you were a girl confesses he's loved you that long as well. With a soaring heart, I join him for the last two stanzas.

> *"Silently and hopelessly I loved you,*
> *At times too jealous and at times too shy.*
> *God grant you find another who will love you*
> *As tenderly and truthfully as I."*

I collapse onto his chest and stare into his warm, blue eyes. "You are the most wonderful man."

"You are the most amazing woman."

Our eyes lock. Our hearts beat together. For a few beautiful seconds, time seems to stop.

"Would you marry me if I asked?" Kirya asks.

"Without a second thought."

He smiles. "I've never been happier than I am right now, in this moment with you," Kirya says, wrapping his arms around me. I burrow into him, resting my head over his heart.

"I feel the same, my love." I close my eyes and take a deep, cleansing breath before letting it out slowly.

After a few minutes, I hear his faint snore. His face is peaceful, content as he sleeps. His mind isn't racing. He's not thinking about protecting me or himself, or what his uncle will ask of him next. I wonder if he ever finds that same serenity when he's awake.

I hope so. I hope he finds it with me. And if he hasn't yet, he will. From this moment on, I will be his peace.

21

KIRYA

*T*he next morning, I wake up at 6:00 a.m., groggily wondering who the fuck set an alarm on our one day to sleep in. We stayed up late last night, reminiscing about life in the communal apartment.

I roll over, stomach still stuffed from the amazing meal Olga filled us with last night.

"It's time to get up, Kirya!" Stasya shakes my shoulder, as if the blaring noise at this ungodly hour wasn't annoying enough. Instead of answer, I growl and try to tug the blanket over me, but she grabs it.

"Come on!" She leans down and drops a kiss on my forehead. "We told *Babushka* we'd help her feed the chickens."

"Shouldn't you feed your man before you feed any chickens," I ask, creeping closer to her. My fingers dance across her thigh before I slide two between her legs. She's already wet, like she woke up ready for me. Like she has every morning since I first touched her here.

The prettiest shade of pink flushes across her cheeks,

turning me on and sparking my fire to continue. "Come on, Stasya. I'm hungry," I say, bringing my finger to my lips and sucking her juices off.

"Then will you get up?" She gasps, but doesn't forget her original mission.

"I'm already up," I say, grabbing my cock. Watching her eyes widen at the sight of my erection will never get old. It's as if she's always surprised at how excited she makes me.

"I guess I'm a little hungry too," she whispers, licking her lips.

My eyes roll to the back of my head and I groan in ecstasy just thinking about her mouth and hands on me. I set my knees on both sides of her shoulders, so her face is right under me. Then I swipe my fingers between her legs and coat my cock with her cum. She watches me circle the tip with hungry eyes, her chest heaving with anticipation.

"You are all I need, Stasya. I will always take care of you."

"We will take care of each other," she says, looking in my eyes as she grabs me. She slides her hands up and down my cock, twisting them in opposite directions as she goes. I've never had anyone do that before and I'm absolutely mesmerized by the feel. It doesn't take her long to find the pressure, speed, and rhythm to get me off, but it feels so good. I don't want it to end.

Collapsing forward, holding myself on my hands above her. I grab my cock, press the tip to her lips, and nudge her mouth open. She accepts me easily, allowing me to slide until I hit the back of her throat.

Using one arm to hold me up, I grab her hair, pulling the roots hard as I buck my hips. She takes hold of the base, guiding every thrust as I fuck her face. The flat part of her tongue presses against my shaft and she groans every time the tip hits her throat.

"Mmmmmmm."

The way she moans and sucks me harder tells me she enjoys it as much as I do.

"Fuck, Stasya! Fuck!" I bat her hand away and take hold again, balls tightening as I jerk my release into her mouth.

It's so hard to keep my eyes open, but I want to watch her take it all. When she's finished, she smiles, lips glistening with cum.

"You are so fucking beautiful," I tell her, pushing the sweaty hair off her forehead.

"Are you still hungry, Kirya?" Her whisper never sounds so sexy as when she's offering her pussy to me to ravish.

"Starving." I slide down and nibble the inside of her thigh, making sure the stubble on my cheek brushes her pussy. She bucks forward, swollen and sensitive where I've touched. "Lay back, my love. I'm going to devour you."

22

STASYA

*A*n overnight in the country with Kirya was exactly what I needed to recharge. I didn't realize how intense owning a business and opening a booth at Cherkizovsky would be. But at least I see the light at the end of the tunnel.

Slava escorts me to the room where about sixty workers sit, bringing my designs to life. I've sat down with each of the people in this room individually, showing them exactly how I want things done.

Kirya purchased the finest fabrics from all over the world. If these clothes are to be my brand, I want every detail to be correct. I'm here daily, inspecting the quality, asking for things to be redone, approving every single piece.

Years ago, when Marina Smirnova made the silly comment about my designs being sold in stores, I'd brushed it off as a fairy tale. But here we are, a few weeks away from opening upstairs—so close I can taste it.

To some, selling clothing at a black market isn't much of an accomplishment, but to me it represents so much more. It's the first step to independence. Though Kirya and I own the business together, he lets me make all the decisions. He calls himself an "investor"—someone who gives money to a project to get it up and running. I appreciate that he sees my talent and thinks I'm good enough to invest in.

I sit next to Yelena, a worker I consider somewhat of a production manager because she speaks Kazakh, which is the language of most of the people sewing my clothing. Despite being part of the USSR, Kazakhstan and its language is completely different from Russia. It sounds stupid, but I've never been there, nor knew much about it, so I honestly didn't realize the differences until I went to speak to someone. Thankfully, Yelena can speak both. She has been a lifesaver in the operation.

We've just started to talk about the newest designs when Igor bursts into the room, surprising all of us.

"Rybakov!" he yells. "Antonov wants you in the Tearoom now."

Slava rushes to the door but pauses uncharacteristically before he leaves. Concern creases his forehead as his head swivels from me to Igor. I understand his hesitation immediately. The conversation Kirya and Slava had about not leaving me alone with Igor is always in the back of my head. Since I've never been alone with him, I assume that's still the rule.

I nod, giving Slava permission to go and tend to whatever Kirya needs. It's not like I'm alone with Igor; I'm in a room full of people.

Igor must notice the exchange because he scowls. "Don't worry, Slava. I always have Stasya's best interest in mind."

My stomach tightens into knots when Slava disappears. While still keeping my guard up, I return to my conversation with Yelena.

Igor flicks through a rack of clothing that's ready to be sold. "Looks nice, Stasya."

"Thank you," I reply trying to sound gracious rather than nervous.

"How's your brother doing?"

My head snaps up, suspicious of his intentions.

Igor and I have never had a conversation. We've been in a group of others talking to each other, but we've never spoken one on one. If Kirya doesn't trust him around me, that's my cue to stay cautious and not interact too much with him.

"I'm sure he's doing fine," I say. "I haven't spoken to him in months."

My relationship with Vanya is almost nonexistent right now. Though I've tried to reach him a few times, he hasn't returned my calls. I wonder if he's too embarrassed or feels too guilty to speak with me. Or maybe he's just too busy living his new life.

Someday we'll be face to face again and we can talk it out. Maybe he'll realize I'm not angry with him, though I *am* hurt at being ignored.

Igor picks up a dress, inspects it, then places it on the rack again. He glances at me. "Don't you think it's weird that Kirya planned your brother's entire defection, yet he hasn't gotten you to America yet?"

"What?" My jaw tightens as I narrow my eyes at him.

He can't be serious. Kirya would have told me if that were true. This must be his way of trying to drive a wedge between us.

"It's funny because he says he cares about you, yes?" He looks at me for confirmation. "If I had a woman I cared about, my first priority would be getting *her* out of Russia not her brother."

I jump up so fast my chair falls to the ground. Not one head in the room looks up, which says a lot about what these people live through every day.

"Did you not know?" Igor asks. "I thought you and your brother were this close." He crosses his middle finger over his index finger. "Hell, I thought you and Kirya were even closer."

His condescending tone makes my blood boil. I can't listen anymore. Without a word of explanation to him or Yelena, I bolt out and sprint to the Tearoom.

Kirya looks up calmly, as if he's unsurprised to see me. "Can I help you?"

"We need to talk," I demand. My chest heaves, fueled by adrenaline and anger.

"I'm busy right now, but I can meet you in a half hour."

"No, Kirya. You will speak with me now." Rage rumbles in my stomach.

Kirya glares at me. He's probably ticked off because I'm making him look bad in front of his business associates, but I couldn't care less.

Finally, he excuses himself and scoots his chair back. He stalks toward me quickly, grabbing my arm and pulling me out of the Tearoom. His face is twisted in anger. Just as he's about to speak, I interrupt him.

"Did you help Vanya get to America?"

The color drains from his face. Anger morphs into guilt. "I did."

"You didn't think to take me with him?"

"No, I didn't. Neither one of us did. It was an extremely tense situation."

The truth cuts into my soul. The two men closest to me. The two men who knew what I'd lived through with Papa. The two men who knew the only thing I ever wanted was to get away. And neither one of them thought of me at all.

Kirya glances at his associates. "No offense, Stasya, but helping an officer in the Scarlet Army defect is hard enough without having another person to worry about while doing it."

I raise my hands, palms up in exasperation. "What about after? Why didn't you send me to the United States to be with him?"

He lowers his tone, speaking softer as if explaining to a child. "Because I can't protect you in the United States."

"I wouldn't have needed protection there." My fists tighten at my side.

He snorts. "You don't think the mafia is there? You don't think they would have done the same thing there as they would have done here?"

Anger burns in my throat. "All this time, I thought you were a saint. But you aren't. You are a selfish man, Kirya."

I turn around, run out the door and up the stairs, and don't stop until I'm lost in the sea of people in the marketplace.

It's while I'm surrounded by shoppers that I realize I'm completely alone for the first time in almost a year. No one watching me. No protection.

Just freedom.

A freedom I had in oppressive, communist Russia before my brother defected. Was my life really so bad? Is having better food and finer clothes worth the freedom I had? Back when I could still take the metro by myself and go dancing with Svetlana without someone lurking in the shadows.

I move with the crowd without having a destination in mind. That's when I see him.

The man with the razor blade smile.

He's walking the aisles, spitting sunflower seeds at the feet of people passing by, like he does every time I see him.

Though I don't know him, I know enough to be on alert

because he's not one of Kirya's men. Instead of letting the crowd carry me along, I elbow and jostle my way through, cutting a right at the aisle where my booth sits empty, waiting for me to fill it with clothes.

Just as I'm about to duck behind the barrier at the back of the booth, someone grabs my arm and jerks me closer to them. "What do you think you're doing?"

"Take your hands off me," I growl in response. I have to force myself to not be intimidated, though his face is scary.

"You must pay to be at this booth."

"I did pay."

He squeezes my arm, tightening his grip to the point of pain. "Maybe you didn't pay the right people."

"Are you implying Kirya Antonov doesn't know the right people to pay?"

He scowls, but loosens his grip slightly. "What do you know about Kirya Antonov?"

"I know enough. I am his wife," I say indignantly.

Maybe it's a lie right now, but I *will* be his wife someday. If being known as his girlfriend tells people they are to respect me, being his wife must be a completely different level. This repulsive thug needs to know who he's dealing with.

"His wife?" he sneers. "Well, that's interesting information."

"Now take your hands off me before—" He releases me before I finish my sentence.

Shoving his hands in his pockets, he teeters from heels to toes nonchalantly. "So," he begins, looking around with a lazy smile before leaning closer, "where is Kirya?"

His sudden, relaxed state puts me on alert.

"Right over there," I say firmly, pointing to an area behind him. When he turns around, I take off the other way, knocking down an old woman in my haste. I don't stop—or even look—to see if she's okay.

This is freedom.

I run directly into a broad chest and stagger back a bit, as if I've bounced off a brick wall. Grimacing, I rub my chin, which was the first thing to hit.

"That was stupid," Kirya says calmly.

"Which part? Running away or running into you?"

"I think we both know the answer." Placing his hand on the small of my back, he leads me through the pack. We're headed toward the parking lot though, not a stairway to the basement.

Slava sits in the BMW, waiting at the edge of the crowd. As we climb in to the car, Kirya asks, "Why are you shaking?"

"I had a run-in with the man who can't stop smiling."

"The man who—" Kirya looks confused.

"The Georgian," Slava interjects, glancing at the rearview mirror.

"Is that his name or where he's from? I assumed he'd be called something like The Joker."

Kirya grabs my hands, bringing me back to the topic. "What kind of run-in?"

"I was at my booth, and he grabbed me and told me I had to pay to be there. So, I told him you know the rules and that I'm your wife."

"What was that last part?"

"I said I was your wife," I repeat quietly, since that seems to have upset him. "I'm sorry, Kirya. I just—" I lower my head and gaze at our hands joined in my lap. "When people find out I'm your girlfriend, they give me respect. I thought he would leave me alone if he thought I was your wife."

Kirya releases me and rubs his face with both hands. He keeps them over his mouth, and blows out a stream of air.

"What did I do wrong?"

He shakes his head to regain his composure, then touches my cheek. "Nothing, my love. You didn't do anything wrong."

He and Slava are uncharacteristically silent the rest of the way home which is unnerving. I can't help but think he's trying to make me feel better, because the tension in the air certainly feels like I fucked up.

23

KIRYA

Slava steps into damage control immediately, stomping the flames of the rumor that I'm married which has been spreading like wildfire throughout the criminal community.

The best thing I can do right now is keep my distance from Stasya. The less she's seen with me, the better.

Now, instead of rushing to get home from my meetings outside Moscow, I stay longer or drive slower. Every second away from her makes me miss her even more.

But staying away isn't enough and no matter what I do, I still don't know how to correct the situation. The one person I've been avoiding since the day I took Stasya into my home is the one person who can help me. The longer I go without calling him, the more danger I put the love of my life in.

I'm sitting on a hard, uncomfortable mattress in an over-priced Leningrad hotel, staring at the phone on the nightstand. My knee bounces up and down as my nerves take control.

"Come on, Kirya, man the fuck up," I scold myself out loud.

Voicing the command gives me courage to lift the handset and dial my uncle's number.

Viktor answers on the third ring. "I'm listening."

"I fucked up," I admit, instead of greeting him.

"What is it? What happened?"

"Stasya got into it with a guy from Sobakin's crew at Cherkizovsky. She told him she was my wife. Now everything is fucked."

"Your wife?" Viktor's voice booms. "Kirya, are you married?"

I rub my forehead with my fingers and close my eyes. "No, but—" My hesitation tells him all he needs to know. According to the State, we may not be married, but we are in my heart and soul.

"When you began this life, I explained *vory* code to you for many reasons. Though I never required you to live by them, I expected you to respect the rules. Especially the ones pertaining to loved ones. You know how much I've feared for my parents, you, and your mother my entire life. You witnessed the lengths I took to keep all of you safe, yes?"

"Yes, sir."

"In taking Miss Kravtsova as your life partner, you chose yourself over her. And that selfishness puts her in grave danger." He pauses. "You've made her fucking target number one now."

He's right. Bringing Stasya into my life was the biggest mistake I could have ever made. If I had been thinking about her best interests instead of my own, I would have sent her to America with Vanya and stayed away. Slava would have hopped on the first plane to Detroit without a second thought if I'd asked him to protect the Kravtsov twins.

"You let your own desires dictate your decisions, which is a strength when it comes to business, but not when it comes to an innocent woman's life."

"I didn't intend for it to happen," I say, but as the words hit the air, I hear the lie.

There's a reason pride is a cardinal sin. It blinded me. I ignored everything I knew, and thought I could defy the odds and keep her safe by having her close.

"You know what you have to do, Kirya." Victor's voice is softer now. "If you truly love Stasya, you must stay away from her."

I lift my eyes to the ceiling and take a deep breath. "Will you help me?"

24

KIRYA

MOSCOW

*I*t's been one week since Viktor and I spoke, and the plan to get Stasya out of Russia is already set. When I told Slava where we were placing her, he had the same reaction I did when my uncle told me.

"You're sending her to Morozov? The only other guy she's fucked?" Slava asks. "Why wouldn't she live with Vanya?"

"Because that's the first place Sobakin will check. It's leading her right to the slaughter."

"Yeah, well, you might be doing that here. Drago said Stasya is all they're talking about. They know taking her out is the best way to get rid of you. They think you'll blow your own brains out if she's dead."

I laugh, but it's not wrong.

If anything happened to Stasya, I wouldn't want to live another day.

I never planned on ever keeping a secret this big from her.

Then again, I never expected to have to send her out of my life forever either. The guilt has been weighing on me and I know she can feel it. In keeping my distance, she fears for our relationship. But staying away from her is the only way to keep quiet.

I can't tell her about the plan to move her to America. She'd refuse to go. She may even do something completely insane, like chain herself to a cross on top of an onion dome on St. Basil's Cathedral. There's a greater chance of everything not going according to plan if she knows.

It feels like I'm helping Vanya escape all over again. The entire trip is planned to the very last detail. I've been ticking things off my list mentally. Slava and Drago know exactly what to do. Her travel documents are set. I've already shipped a box of things to her new residence so they'll be there when she arrives. There's a black backpack loaded with clothes and toiletries she'll need for the flight in the trunk of the car.

The only thing left to do is kiss my love goodbye.

* * *

ON THE MORNING OF HER FLIGHT, I WAKE HER IN HER FAVORITE way—with my cock sliding into her pussy. She reacts the same way every time I press myself into her ass, wiggling and grinding into me. That's how I know she's awake and ready to accept me. She's always ready to accept me.

I reach between us, line up my cock, and push into her.

She sighs.

My arm snakes around her stomach, bringing her as close as possible, and I press my lips to her neck. I breathe in deeply, memorizing her sweet scent of lavender and sweat from the sex we had last night. I'm going to miss everything about her.

Every. Fucking. Thing.

My fingers move to her clit, rubbing it as I keep up my slow, rhythmic thrusts. She moans and presses into me, her breath catching as I move faster. Four fingers up and down then two fingers in circles—switching it up in the cadence she loves until she explodes all over me.

Kissing her shoulder, I slide out of her and out of bed, giving her time to enjoy the orgasm in her sleepy haze. I go to the bathroom to clean up before making my way to the kitchen to make her breakfast.

Stasya shuffles in about a half hour later, wearing my favorite outfit: disheveled sex hair and one of my white button-down shirts.

"Do you have any plans today?" I ask, scooping a soft-boiled egg out of the saucepan and delicately placing it into an egg holder.

She stretches her arms above her head, giving me full view of her naked body. "It feels like I haven't seen you in forever, Kirya," she says after a yawn. "I think we should spend the day in bed."

She sits at the kitchen table, folding one leg under her. I let my gaze linger, taking in the curve of her neck and the way she always seems to glow in the sunlight streaming through the windows.

"Not today, my love. I have a surprise." I bring her breakfast to the table and hand her a spoon. She accepts it, lifting a piece of buttered rye from a plate of toast in front of her, as I give her a wink. "We're going for a walk down memory lane."

"Really?" she asks with an interested smile.

"Yes. And I'm going to quiz you on your English," I tease. "So, you better grab that dictionary from your desk."

"Do I have time to finish my breakfast?" she asks.

"Yes. Fill your stomach, my love. But be quick, because I'm going to fill your pussy once more before we go."

* * *

Within a hour, we're standing on the street in front of the communal apartment we grew up in together. Memories of all the laughter and tears during the time we spent here flood my mind. Emotion makes words stick in my throat.

"You have many bad memories of this place, I know. But there's only one thing I want you to remember." I lift her chin so our gazes meet. "This is where we met. And if we never met, I would have never known what it feels like to truly know love."

She smiles. "Kirya—"

"I need you to know, Stasya, my love. Everything I do is because I love you. You may not understand. You may not agree, but you know…" I place my hand on her chest. "In here, you've always known that I act out of love."

She places her hand on my heart. "You know the same about me."

"I was put on this earth for you."

I'm not expecting Slava yet when he screeches to a stop in front of us.

"We need to move now, Kirya! Sobakin is on his way. Two cars," he yells through the open window.

Stasya begins to shake. "Kirya? What's going on?"

I've planned murders. I've shot people in cold blood without a second thought.

Yet here I am, about to lose my shit.

Stasya is the only person who has ever been able to penetrate my hardened heart.

"You trust me, yes?" I ask, my eyes pleading with hers.

"With every bone in my body," she says firmly, without hesitation.

I sweep my thumb across her cheek, which is already a bright red from the frigid wind against her exposed skin. "You must trust me once more, or you won't survive."

"Once more?" Her eyes glaze over. "Kirya, what does that mean? What's going on?"

I grab her by the shoulders, squeezing until she lifts her glassy eyes to mine. "Have I ever hurt you?"

She pauses and blinks, which releases a tear, then shakes her head. "No."

"Listen to me and you will be safe. I promise you, my love." I release her shoulders and grab her cheeks, hoping the bond in our gaze ensures I'm getting through to her. "You have your dictionary, yes?"

She nods, her knuckles white as she clutches the thick straps of the backpack resting on her shoulder, adjusting them slightly. Her bottom lip trembles and she squeezes her eyes closed. Tears cascade down her cheeks.

Sobakin's black BMW with two red racing stripes across the hood rounds the corner followed by an Escalade in the same shade, sans stripes. My heart pounds in my ear, ticking like the second hand on a clock.

"Anastasiya," I say firmly when she tries to lower her head. The fear on her face breaks my heart, but reinforces my decision. She can't be part of this life any longer. Her beautiful soul can't bear any more loss—and mine can't bear losing her. "Don't look back. Do you understand me?"

She nods again.

My eyes flick to the street behind her, where the cars creep closer.

Tick. Tick. Tick.

Fuck.

"Do *not* look back," I whisper harshly, drawing her into my arms and hugging her tighter than I ever have.

After a life of getting everything I want when I want it, letting go of the only thing I've ever needed kills me.

Stasya is the only woman I ever loved. The only person I would give my life to protect.

Which is why I have to get her the hell away from me.

Reluctantly, I let go and hold her at arm's length, taking in her beautiful features for a second too long. A river of tears slide down her face and drip onto her jacket, dotting it with drops.

That's the last image I have of my Stasya.

Cheeks red from the harsh Moscow winds, big, blue eyes wide with fear, and tears gliding down her cheeks.

25

STASYA

*A*nother black BMW pulls up, tires screeching as it slows down next to us. The window on the passenger side is already down—a long barrel poking out.

I'm frozen with fright, unable to move.

A rapid succession of gunshots explode in my ear.

Kirya pushes me hard and jumps into the spray of bullets.

I stumble backward into Slava's thick chest. He locks his arms around me and drags me away. My heart hammers so hard, I feel like it might break out of my ribcage.

I watch in terror as Kirya's body hits the ground.

"No!" I scream. "No!"

Twisting and thrashing, I struggle with every ounce of strength I have to get away, but Slava's fingers don't budge, digging deeper into my arms and dragging me backward.

The puddle of blood forming underneath Kirya's body is the last thing I see before my face slides across a leather seat as I'm shoved headfirst into the back of the car.

End Book i

This epic story continues in SINNERS

Leaving Kirill behind wasn't my choice.
But he sacrificed everything to get me to America, and I'm determined to make him proud.

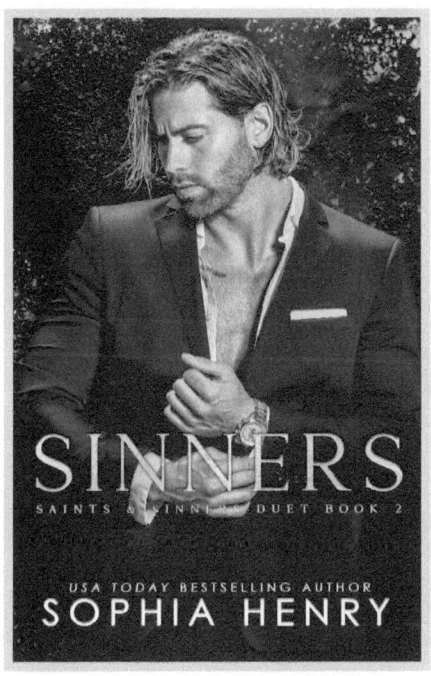

After a few years, I've finally settled into my new normal—running a successful business and rekindling a relationship with a former flame.

I thought I'd left the mafia in Moscow, but when the head of operations in New York is murdered, a new leader emerges—and turns the life I've built upside down.

The line between Saint and Sinner has never been so blurry, but deep down, I've always known which side I'd end up on.

Sinners is the 2nd book in the Saints and Sinners Duet and should NOT be read before Saints. One Click this gripping, romantic suspense today!

READ SINNERS NOW!

Lace up your skates and keep your eye on the puck, it's time to hit the ice in USA Today Bestseller Sophia Henry's Aviators Hockey Series!

Find out why New York Times Bestselling Author Rachel Harris raves, "The romance is off the charts and Sophia Henry tackles real issues that tug at your heartstrings."

DELAYED PENALTY: Enemies-to-Lovers Romance
An Aviators Hockey Novel

Losing my soccer scholarship left me scrambling to find a way to afford my college tuition. Thankfully, I landed a gig as a translator for a minor-league Russian hockey player.

Sadly, the initial enthusiasm was short lived.

One glance and I immediately recognized my new client as

the same arrogant jerk who came on to me at the bar the night before. Sure, Aleksandr Varenkov was sexy--with his chiseled muscles and alluring grin. That didn't change the fact that he's a notorious womanizer.

While our working relationship started as friendly as a hard check on the ice, I soon saw a softer side to Aleksandr that left me entertaining thoughts of a trip for two to the penalty box.

After all I've been through, I can't risk letting my guard down for a hot-headed player with a bad reputation. Still... how can I resist an attraction hot enough to melt the ice?

Delayed Penalty is hailed as "sexy, fun, and full of angst" by New York Times and USA Today Best Selling author L. P. Dover.

Turn the page for a Sneak Peek of DELAYED PENALTY

DELAYED PENALTY EXCERPT

CHAPTER 1
AUDEN

When you're twenty years old, there's nothing music and a drink can't cure.

At least that was my best friend's response when I told her I'd been cut from Central State's women's soccer team this morning.

The overzealous stylings of two drunk chicks bellowing "It's Raining Men" wafts through the air, and I've just received my vodka club from the bartender. So why does it still feel like someone scratched my heart out with a serrated shovel?

Maybe "It's Raining Men" isn't the right song?

Or maybe my friend's remedy lacked one vital ingredient.

Like, five minutes locked in a bathroom stall with the crazy-haired hottie approaching me. His head is buzzed short on the sides, leaving a thick patch of dark locks, gelled into a neat pompadour in front. Sort of like a 1920s gangster, except less slicked, more height.

Every muscle in Crazy Hair's body ripples under his clothing as he walks. He has to be over six feet tall, with a broad chest and massive arms stretching the seams of his long-sleeved black Henley. His smooth, pale skin is a contrast to the thick dark eyebrows resting above his jump-in-and-drown-in-me blue eyes. From the scar on his left cheek to the smug smirk of his lips, he looks exactly my type: dangerous, confident, and totally lickable.

I flip my long blond hair behind my shoulder and glance to my left, pretending Crazy Hair's advance has no effect on me. In reality, I'm checking to make sure he isn't about to pass me up on the way to some beautiful bombshell I hadn't noticed standing in the vicinity.

Like when you see someone wave, so you wave back. Then you realize they weren't waving at you but the person behind you. Then you try to play off your lame wave like you were batting away mosquitoes—which aren't there because it's December in Canada.

Just trying to avoid an awkward situation like that.

Crazy Hair continues to close in, before stopping just inches away.

I open my mouth to ream him out for stepping too far into my personal space, but the sweet scent of clove cigarettes floods warmth through me like a sip of steaming hot chocolate on a January morning in the Upper Peninsula.

"You work at post office?" he asks in a thick Slavic accent.

"Um, no." I take a swig of my drink. Though I'm unsure where he's going with that line, he's hot enough for me to stick around.

The left corner of his mouth curves into that sexy little smirk. "Because I see you check out my package."

Carbonation stings my nose as I snort and choke trying to hold in my laugh. Without time to turn my head, I spray vodka club and saliva across the front of Crazy Hair's shirt.

Awesome.

"Weak!" I hear from somewhere behind me.

I turn to see who had yelled, still coughing as I notice a group of guys and girls at the high-top table behind me. Shaggy blond hair bounces against one guy's forehead as he snickers. The dude next to him holds his fist in front of his mouth in a horrible attempt to hide his laughter. A brunette in a tight red sweater doesn't look amused. At all.

Crazy Hair throws the guys not one—but both—of his middle fingers.

"That girl's a fucking smoke show. Why'd he use a shitty line like that?" the blond one asks.

Smoke show? I bite down hard on my lip to fight back a smile. The last time I'd heard that phrase was in high school from my hockey-playing best friend, who'd informed me that "smoke show" was player lingo for "hot girl."

Unsure of how to recover any semblance of cool after spitting my drink across Crazy Hair's muscular chest, I spin around and shuffle back to the table my friends occupied in front of the karaoke stage.

It feels weird to drink in public, though we've been to Canada on multiple occasions. As lifelong residents of Detroit, Michigan, we think of Windsor—the Canadian city connected to Detroit by a bridge and a tunnel—as the next town over, rather than a foreign country. Nineteen is the legal drinking age in Windsor, so it makes sense that underage Americans like us cross the border for some legit cocktails.

My butt barely brushes my seat when I hear my name, and my name alone, called over the speakers. I lift my eyes to the outdated popcorn ceiling, as if the voice is resonating from the heavens beyond, rather than the karaoke host.

"Why is he calling my name?" I ask Kristen.

"I picked you a song," she responds, then tips her beer back.

"You picked *us* a song, you mean?" Emphasis on the us, because I've never sung alone in my life—not counting the shower and car, of course.

"Nope. Just you." Kristen places both hands on my back and pushes me toward the stage. "You need to sing it out. Keeping shit bottled up never works."

I wouldn't have a problem singing it out if I were singing with other people, but just me? Haven't I been embarrassed enough today?

My short-lived "smoke show" happiness vanishes, and the embarrassment of making a fool of myself in front of Crazy Hair returns. I try to reverse, but Kristen's trampoline-like hands propel me back toward the stage.

Climbing onto the stage, I snatch the microphone out of the host's hand. I almost feel bad about taking my anger out on him until I see the lyrics to "Proud Mary" light up in white against the teleprompter's blue screen. Fuck.

What the hell? I exhale and lift my eyes to Kristen.

"Girl power!" She salutes me with her glass.

Is "Proud Mary" a girl-power song? I thought it was about a boat.

"Do you have 'Good Feeling'?" I ask the karaoke host. He's around my age, with big brown eyes that match his neat, trimmed beard and shoulder-length hair.

"Flo Rida?" he asks, as disapproving wrinkles form on his smooth forehead.

"Oh, no," I say, shaking my head. "The Violent Femmes."

A smile spreads across his lips, and he nods. "Give me a second."

While waiting for my song, I take in the scenery at Mickey O'Callaghan's Irish Pub. The space itself is cozy; small and narrow with red and beige brick walls and mahogany overkill. The dark wood is everywhere—the long bar, the wainscoting, the narrow beams on the ceiling, even the tables and chairs. Evidently Mickey's is the place to be for Friday-night karaoke, because bodies occupy every seat, and the bar is two people deep all the way across.

Instead of looking toward the table Crazy Hair threw double birds to earlier, I watch the karaoke host fiddle with his machine. After a minute, the screen glows with the lyrics to my request.

My voice cracks delivering the first note, causing my cheeks to burn. I keep my eyes glued to the teleprompter, even though I know the words by heart. After the first few lines, I get my vocals on track, and I hear some clapping, which surprises me. Halfway through the song, I lift my eyes to see people on their feet—people other than the friends I had come with—although my friends are on their feet as well. By the time I finish the song, the crowd is hooting and whistling. Someone yells for me to sing again, but I just smile as I refasten the microphone to the stand.

"You were amazing, Aud!" Kristen squeezes me when I get back to the table.

"I didn't know you could sing like that." Lacy raises her hand for a high five.

"I didn't either," I admit, skimming my palm against hers, sure I'd zap her with the electricity tingling through my limbs.

Being on stage felt like overtime at a soccer match: exhilarating and exciting.

"Hey," someone says, tapping my shoulder. I spin around to see the karaoke host.

"Greg." He thrusts his hand at me.

"Auden," I say, taking his outstretched palm. "Thanks for switching songs."

"Tina Turner didn't seem like your thing." Greg might've had a cute face hiding under his beard. Still not my type, though. Too monotone. Even the plaid flannel hanging off his lean frame is brown. His style screams Eddie-Vedder-nineties-grunge rather than today's hipster cool.

"Oh, I can rock some Tina. Just wasn't feeling 'Proud Mary' without my backup singers." I point to Kristen and Lacy.

Greg laughs. "Need a drink?"

"I already have—" I search the table for my drink, spotting it in Lacy's boyfriend's hand. "Actually, I do."

Ignoring Kristen's megawatt smile, I follow Greg to the bar. She better not have set him on me to boost my spirits. She knows he isn't my type. Douche bags like Crazy Hair and the guys he'd flipped off got my motor running. Douche bags and I are on the same wavelength. Neither of us want more than what the other could offer.

Greg moves to the side so I can order. "Club soda with three limes, please."

"And a Steam Whistle." Greg points to a beer I don't recognize in the stand-up cooler behind the bar. The bartender nods and extracts a bottle.

"You've got a killer voice," Greg says.

"Well, there're no Tina Turner–type vocals in that song." I blow off his compliment.

"No, but it's hard to sing that soft and keep your key." His mouth curves into a wide, kind smile. "You from around here?"

"Detroit," I say, nodding. "But I go to Central State."

"Are you kidding?"

I shake my head and pick up the drink the bartender placed in front of me.

"So do I. That's crazy." Greg holds up a few bills, waiting until the bartender sees the money before setting it on the bar. "My roommates and I have a band and we're looking for a singer right now."

"You're in a band? That's awesome," I say, focused on mashing the limes in my drink. I raise my glass to him. "Thank you, by the way."

"No problem." He picks at the label on his beer bottle. "Any interest?"

"In what?" I ask, looking at Greg over the top of my cup.

"Singing for our band." He doesn't even blink.

"You're joking, right?" I laugh. Asking me to sing in his band after hearing one karaoke song was hilarious. I've never taken voice lessons, and as far as I can tell, I don't have any significant talent.

"Why would I joke?" He doesn't seem to understand my laughter at all.

"I just sang in public for the first time and you're asking me if I want to be in a band?" Being the center of attention for five minutes in a karaoke bar is one thing; standing on stage in front of people expecting a show is a different beast.

"So that explains your lack of stage presence," Greg says, running his fingers over his beard, looking more English professor than rocker.

"Quite the charmer, aren't you, G-man?" I take a drink. I

know I don't have stage presence. Hell, I couldn't even make eye contact with anyone.

"Stage presence can be learned," he says. "You have a great voice and a hot look."

Once I realize he's not kidding, I'm speechless.

Greg continues peeling the label off his beer bottle as he waits for me to speak. "It's nothing crazy. We just play bars in Bridgeland, well, mostly at Wreckage." He chuckles.

"Yeah, I don't think so, but thanks for asking." I force a half smile.

"Come on," he pleads. "Just try out. If you like it, great."

"I don't think I could even learn to be comfortable on stage."

"I can get you over your stage fright." Greg's voice is molasses, thick and smooth; a contrast to his grunge-hipster vibe. The lights flickering above give his previously plain eyes a sexy sparkle as he waits for my answer.

Why do I have to be a sucker for sparkles? "Okay, sure." My head bobs in reluctant consent. "The worst that could happen is I fail miserably, right?"

"I don't know. You might surprise me." Greg winks. He searches the bar before grabbing a pen lying on an abandoned credit card receipt. Then he flips over a coaster advertising some brewing company's winter ale and begins scribbling. "Here's my number. Call me next week for an audition."

"This is crazy." I take the coaster from him.

"What do you have to lose?" His eyes are solid and intense as he stares at me.

Nothing. I'd long since lost it all. But he doesn't know that.

Without another word, he walks away, leaving me alone at the bar, perplexed by the interaction.

"What did Eddie Vedder's son have to say?" Kristen asks, nodding toward Greg, who's resumed his place behind the karaoke machine. Of course, Kristen would think of a similar description for his look. It's one of the many reasons we'd been calling each other our 'other half" since the first day of freshman year when we were assigned to the same dorm room.

"He wants to me to try out for his band," I say, flashing her the coaster. "Which is stupid."

"No, it isn't." She snatches my hand and squeezes. "You're really good."

I shake my head. Right now, I'm high from my time on stage and the applause and compliments I'd received, but as soon as I get home and start over-analyzing the unexpected conclusion to my soccer career again, the euphoria will abandon me. Just like my team had.

Just like everyone does.

"You're a popular lady tonight. The Mohawked hottie stared at you the entire time you talked to karaoke guy."

I follow Kristen's gaze to the table where Crazy Hair and his friends are sitting. Though the group seems to be leaving, downing their drinks and grabbing their coats, Crazy Hair stands still, his penetrating eyes on me.

I have a feeling he's the type of guy who would say anything to get me to take him home, and then slink away without a word the next morning. Though drinking has usually been involved when that had happened, I can't even blame the alcohol. I fall for guys like him because I need the attention. I need to feel like someone wants me. I need to pretend that someone might be able to love me.

The way my parents should have loved me.

It's an impossible void to fill.

Crazy Hair slides one of the muscular arms I'd admired earlier around the shoulders of the girl with the tight red sweater. She has big everything; big hair, big boobs, big smile.

Still holding my gaze, he says something against her ear, which makes her throw her head back in a laugh revealing big white teeth. Sliding his hand down her back, he allows her to go first as they follow the rest of the group toward the door.

Which reminds me of another definition of smoke show: to dominate, crush, or otherwise humiliate the opposition.

Mission accomplished.

Douche.

START READING DELAYED PENALTY NOW!

REVIEWS ROCK!

THANK YOU so much for taking the time to read SAINTS! I truly appreciate every single one of you. If you enjoyed reading SAINTS as much as I enjoyed writing it, it would mean the world to me if you would consider leaving a review on Amazon.

(Really love me? Copy and paste the same review to Bookbub & Goodreads!)

DON'T FORGET to grab **SINNERS**, the final installment of the Saints and Sinners Duet!

DON'T MISS OUT!
GET ALL THE SOPHIA HENRY NEWS!

Sophia Henry's mailing list is the place to be if you like steamy romance novels that tug at your heart strings. Stay notified of new releases, sales, exclusive content with newsletters twice a month. Get a FREE book when you sign up at sophiahenry.com.

* * *

JOIN SOPHIA'S READER GROUP

When you join Sophia's Patreon Community you get exclusive access to AUDIO of her books, get sneak peeks, exclusive posts, and extra surprises just for members. You even get to name characters! (Seriously, it happens. Sophia's readers named Zayne, the hero of CRAZY FOR YOU).
Join the Fun: patreon.com/sophiahenry313

* * *

MERCH STORE

Choose kindness and love with everything you've got. It's not just a motto. It's a way of life. Grab some motivational or bookish merch today! www.bekindlovehard.com

PLAYLIST

COMPLETE PLAYLIST ON YOUTUBE:
SOPHIAHENRYOFFICIAL

Don't Let Me Down – The Chainsmokers feat. Daya
On Fire – Sebadoh
Break Your Heart – The Gaslight Anthem
Treat You Better– Rüfüs Du Sol
You Sang To Me – Marc Anthony
Sit Down – James
Million Bucks - Smallpools
I Feel You – Depeche Mode
Here With Me – Marshmello, Chvrches
Shake It Out – Manchester Orchestra
Tonight Tonight – Mondo Cozmo
Drive That Fast – Kitchens of Distinction
With Me All Along – Bronze Radio Return
2all – Catfish and the Bottlemen
Wait For It – Leslie Odom Jr, Original Broadway Cast of
Hamilton
I Always Wanna Die Sometimes – The 1975
Hurt Like Hell – The Heydaze

Hurricane 2.0 – Thirty Seconds to Mars feat. Kanye West
Get Hurt – The Gaslight Anthem
Just Say Yes – Snow Patrol
Surrender – Walk the Moon
This Kind Of Love– Sister Hazel
Good Things Fall Apart – Illenium with Jon Bellion
Skinny Love – Bon Iver
Pray For Me – Smallpools
Feel Good – Daya, Gryffin, Illenium
You Can't Tell How Much Suffering – James
Get Out – Frightened Rabbit
Burn – Usher
I Would Die 4 U – Prince

Note From the Author
Regarding Historical Accuracy and
Creative License

Dear Beautiful Reader,

I wrote the Saints and Sinners Duet as a 20th Century Historical Fiction novel after 25+ years of research and passion for Russian people and their culture—history, sports (hockey), literature, language, etc.

In some cases, I changed names (even historically accurate and important names). For example: I chose to call the army and hockey team the Central Scarlet Army. While "Red" Army is historically accurate and has a deep and meaningful place in Soviet history, there is still a Red Army hockey team (in the form of HC CSKA Moscow). Due to copyright laws, the risk of a Cease and Desist letter, or being sued (ouch!!), I choose not to use real team names when I use a likeness of the team in fiction. It's the same mindset as when I create fictional NHL or AHL teams.

I chose "Scarlet," not because I think it is interchangeable with "Red," but for the reasons I mentioned above. It's my preference to use a fictional name. I also liked the alliteration. It sounds pretty paired with the "S" sound at the beginning of Central. Don't you think? :)

This duet was written with the utmost respect and appreciation for Russian people and their beautiful history and culture.

Thank you so much for your support!

Sending you love and light.

Happy Reading!

ACKNOWLEDGMENTS

First, I want to acknowledge YOU! Thank you for picking my books, reading them, recommending them to others, and for all of your kind messages. It means the world to me. Thank you! Thank you! YOU ROCK!!

My boys, Boo Boo and Chachi: You two are my heart. Even though I write for a living, I don't have words to express how much I love you. I appreciate every second of every single day with you. You continue to inspire me and show me how to be a better person. Thank you for being proud of me.

Jenn Wood and Jackie Ferrell: You two author-lifesavers have done it again!! Thank you all for always being willing to help and for the amazing advice and edits. I truly appreciate how each of you helped shape this into an amazing story and how you polished this book to make me look like an English pro. I'm so grateful your keen eyes catch the areas where I trip up.

Terra Kelly and Jessica Peterson: Thank you. I love the days we get together to write, chat, vent, and just hang out. I truly value your opinions and honesty, and appreciate how wonderful you are at kicking my butt into shape, while still being kind. I feel very lucky to have two amazing humans as part of my local support system. Thank you for being amazing friends and encouraging me to keep reaching for the next goal.

Wander Aguiar, Zach Salaun: I'm humbled and grateful to

have had the chance to work with such extremely talents artists. I appreciate you for helping me bring the *Saints* cover to life.

The phenomenal staff at Amélie's French Bakery. Years ago, I was drawn in by the delicious food and tasty drinks, but I return for the wonderful people and eclectic, all-encompassing, positive vibe. Thanks to everyone for creating a space where anyone can come in, sit down, and feel comfortable as I get my work done.

I'm extremely grateful to have phenomenal friends: I will always take a moment to thank my #TZWNDUBC peeps and original RT ladies because I couldn't imagine my life without your encouragement and support. I'm proud to call each one of you my friend, and appreciate that you've always accepted me as I am, no matter what stage of my life.

Every author, reader, blogger, and friend I've connected with in the writing world: This truly is an amazing community of people who build up their peers to help each other succeed. I'm so fortunate to be part of such a supportive environment.

ALSO BY SOPHIA HENRY

***

<u>FOREIGN EDITIONS</u>

<u>FRENCH</u>
SAGA MATERIAL GIRLS
OPEN YOUR HEART

LIVE TO TELL

CRAZY FOR YOU

DEVIL IN DISGUISE

DUO SAINTS AND SINNERS
SAINTS

SINNERS

ROMANS AUTONOMES LIÉS AUX SAGAS
EVEN STRENGTH

Saints & Sinners/Aviators Hockey Crossover Novel

SAGA AVIATORS HOCKEY
JINGLE BALL BENDER

BLUE LINES

***

<u>GERMAN</u>
MATERIAL GIRLS SERIES
OPEN YOUR HEART

LIVE TO TELL

CRAZY FOR YOU

* * *

RUSSIAN

SAINTS AND SINNERS SERIES

SAINTS

SINNERS

ABOUT THE AUTHOR

USA Today Bestselling Author Sophia Henry is a proud Detroit native who fell in love with reading, writing, and hockey all before she became a teenager. After graduating with a Creative Writing degree from Central Michigan University, she moved to warm and sunny North Carolina where she spent twenty glorious years before heading back to her roots and settling in Michigan.

She spends her days writing steamy, heartfelt contemporary romance and posting personal stories in her Patreon community hoping they resonate with and encourage others. When Sophia's not writing, she's hanging out with her two high-energy sons, an equally high-energy Plott Hound, and two cats who want nothing to do with any of them. She can also be found watching her beloved Detroit Red Wings and rocking out at as many concerts as she can possibly attend.

Receive a FREE ebook and get all the latest releases and updates exclusively for readers! Subscribe to Sophia's newsletter today. https://bit.ly/FreeSHBookNL

www.ingramcontent.com/pod-product-compliance
Lightning Source LLC
Chambersburg PA
CBHW022013170626
46808CB00001B/379